M.T. DESANTIS

Critical Hit-On

The Games of Love, #1

This book was originally published in 2015 with different cover art under the author name Deanna Dee.

Kit 'n Kabookle Literary, LLC

https://kitnkabookle.com

New Cover Design by GetCovers.com

Editing by Stephanie Parent

Second edition

ISBN: 978-1-962838-02-3

This book was professionally typeset on Reedsy.
Find out more at reedsy.com

For the geek in all of us, and in loving memory of Douglas Adams.
42

Contents

Chapter 1: Craig

For a Thursday night, A's Tavern is dead. All the better. We don't need an audience for the not-so-drunken debauchery to follow. I stroll inside and head for the hostess desk, figuring Parker will grab the door before it swings and hits him. He's a big boy. He can handle himself.

There's a crash behind me, followed by a string of what might pass for cursing on an alien planet.

Or not. Oh, Parker. But seriously, how hard is it to catch a door before it hits you? Like the good friend I am, I snicker a little before making sure he's okay.

Parker finishes calling the door names and then faces me, eyes narrowing. "Are you engaging in laughter at my expense? You, my friend, are chimera excrement."

That's Parker-speak for lots of unflattering things. "Hey, I made sure you were okay."

"Two?" Thankfully, Parker's response is interrupted by the host, who's clad in black pants and a signature red shirt for the recent *Star Trek* movie—poor bastard.

"For now," I say. "We're expecting three more."

Host pauses, and his eyes go glassy as if two plus three is calculus. Then he grabs five menus and bundles of silverware.

1

"Follow me." He leads us to a rectangular table for six, where he practically drops everything. Dude's dexterity score is down with his math skills. "Your server will be right with you," he says and then scurries back toward the front of the restaurant.

I mumble a *thanks* and sit. The tables around us are empty, so I pull my chair way out and make myself comfortable. In my twenty-one years, A's hasn't changed. The place looks like one of those old train stations. The top halves of the walls are white tile, and the bottoms are dark wood, a match for the tables and chairs. Monochrome tiles make up the floor, and a black-lacquered bar stretches the length of the restaurant. In honor of the recent *Star Trek* movie, there's a neon sign over said bar advertising Free Tranya. I don't know why they have free tranya, considering that line was from the original series and not the most recent movie, but there's the sign. Only the second r is out. So it reads Free Tanya.

"Free Tanya." Parker sits across from me and runs a hand over his black hair, which just makes it stick up more. Between that and the glasses, all he needs is green eyes instead of blue and a lightning scar on his forehead. "Someone, such as myself, should inform them their sign is incorrect."

Oh, please, no. I scoot up to the table and am about to seize his arm to keep him sitting when a hand grabs my water glass and scares the crap out of me. I hit the back of my chair and look up at our waitress … our really hot waitress. Whoa, how have I not noticed this girl before? Her brown hair reaches her shoulders, and her curves actually make the A's server uniform flattering. My kind of girl.

"How you boys doing tonight?" she says in a strong, confident voice.

Definitely my kind of girl.

"Magnificently," Parker says.

"Yeah?" She replaces my water glass and goes for Parker's. "What can I get you to drink?"

Parker points to the bar. "I shall have the free Tanya, which should—."

I kick him under the table.

He squeaks like a little girl. "I'll have the Tranya."

Waitress nods as if she deals with Parker's brand of dorky twenty-something guy all the time. "And you?" She turns to me, and her brown eyes meet mine. They're the kind of eyes dead white guys wrote poetry about.

I'll be a dead white guy someday. Perhaps I should join their ranks. Or perhaps I should order a drink before she notices I'm staring. "Have you had the tranya?"

"I have. I relished it."

Whoa, girl knows her *Star Trek*. That decides my drink order. "As much as I will."

Her eyes go wide, reflecting my amazement. Then, without warning, they're serious again. "Two tranyas. Can I see some ID?" She barely glances at the cards before handing them back. "I'll have those right out, and my name's Molly." She dashes toward the bar.

Well, so much for that.

"Critical miss," Parker says, patting my arm. "Better luck next time."

I snap out of my daze. "You're a critical miss." But I'm prevented from further insult by a tap on my shoulder.

"Now, now, Craig, be nice to Parker." Lyd slides into the seat next to me. Her brown hair, as per normal, is in a tight braid, and her blue eyes are mischievous. "No matter how difficult that may be."

3

"You mean impossible?" Sonya flops into the chair next to Parker.

I blink at her. "What is in your hair?"

She turns, revealing a pair of dragon chopsticks holding a spiral shape she's managed to make her auburn curls form. "In honor of tonight's festivities. Expect my ponytail back tomorrow." She plants her elbows on the table. "So, we miss anything?"

"Craig attempted to make casual romantic advances on our waitress," Parker says. "It was rather amusing."

Warmth climbs my cheeks. "You know what else is rather amusing? You ordering—"

"Enough, children." Dawn stands at the head of the table like some vengeful motorcycle goddess, tote bag slung over one shoulder. The streak of violet in her black hair glows in the overhead lights. When we're all looking at her, she takes a seat and hauls the bag into her lap. "Thank you for being punctual."

"Says she who has arrived late," Parker says.

Dawn gives him a one-eyed stare that many a strong man has cowered from. "I'm in charge of you, starting now. I may arrive whenever I please." She pulls a five-inch binder out of the tote, setting it down and opening it in one motion.

Sonya leans forward, and somehow, the mysterious hairdo stays in place. "Are those them?"

Dawn nods. "Your character sheets." She extracts four packets from the binder and hands one to each of us. "Welcome to our first campaign session."

There are a few moments of silence as we flip pages. We all pitched in to help Dawn pay for a subscription to Marshalls and Magics' online system, figuring it made the most sense for the game master to have access. Then we gave her our character stats in exchange for official character sheets. Mine is as I specified—hawk spirit shaman wereclaw shifter. Yup, I'm one kickass, ugly healer.

"Wait a minute." Parker tosses his packet on the table. "You horrid Game master. We're having our first session in a tavern?"

Lyd and Sonya's heads pop up like hellhounds who've caught the scent of prey.

"Literally *A Tavern*," Sonya says. "The hell? Are we larping this bad boy?"

"No," Dawn says, not looking up. "We are not live action role playing, and before you ask, we are not changing location. I am the GM. I am God. What I say goes."

We fall silent. While all that is true, it's not the reason we don't object. None of us has a desire to take on a five-foot-eight woman in black leather and combat boots with more tattoos than plain skin and piercings in places holes should not be made. Our one sign of collective intelligence.

"That's better." Dawn stops flipping pages and gives us her attention, gray eyes serious. "Now, while we are, in fact, seated in a tavern, you will not be starting in a tavern." She licks her lips. "You'll be starting—"

"Three more?" Molly places two glasses of amber liquid on the table. "What would you ladies like to drink?"

I pull the tranya toward me and take a sniff. Scotch and cherries? No, the cherry isn't coming from the glass. It's coming from Molly, which I enjoy for a second before stopping. Talk about being a creep. Oops.

The girls order drinks—Sonya a lemonade, Lyd cranberry juice, and Dawn water.

"I'll be right back with those," Molly says but doesn't take her gaze from the table. Curiosity flits in her eyes before her expression clamps down.

My personal air bubble of attractive waitress pops. I've seen that look too many times to count. It's the girl-just-discovered-guy-is-more-of-a-dork-than-she-thought look. So much for my attempts at flirting.

"I'll be right back," Molly says and takes her leave.

"You're right. Craig trying to flirt is funny." Sonya gives me a pitying headshake. "Talking usually helps."

Dawn taps one red fingernail on the center of the table. "Moving on. Are your characters correct?"

There's a chorus of *yes*, mine included, if a bit slower than the rest.

"Excellent," Dawn says. "Now, the beginning. As I said, you will not be starting in a tavern. You will be starting in a bar."

Chapter 2: Molly

relished it? Where the hell did that come from?

I race away from the table with the gorgeous blond-haired, green-eyed, square-jawed … stop it. He's a customer, and I will know him only as guy-named-Craig, guy-named-Craig who responded to my *Star Trek* reference, which has never happened, ever. Is he a hard-core Trekker? No, focus. He knows *Star Trek,* which means he's a geek, which means he probably plays video games in his mother's basement. You don't do guys who play video games in their mothers' basements.

"Earth to Molly." Nikki, my coworker and best friend, waves a pink-nailed hand in front of my face.

"What?" I don't remember charging into the kitchen and slumping against the wall. Nevertheless, that's where I am. I straighten and swat Nikki's hand away. "What did I miss?"

Nikki runs her fingers through her blonde ponytail. "Nothing. But if you don't get drinks for table fifteen soon, you're going to be missing a tip."

That's right. I have to get guy-named-Craig his tranya that he'll relish. Really, Molls, snap out of it. No way am I going anywhere near that table. "Do you think you could—"

"No. I don't think I could. Your table. Your drinks."

Crap. What am I going to do? I can't go back over there. I'm liable to do something stupid, like encourage guy-named-Craig to hit on me. Wait, that's it. "But one of those guys hit on me."

Nikki freezes, and her eyes narrow. Smoke might even come out of her ears. There is no greater restaurant patron sin in her mind then hitting on a waitress. "Did he, now? We'll just see about that." She sashays to the door.

I let out a breath. Thank the pantheon that worked. Yes, I should feel like a bad friend for pulling the pet-peeve card, but I don't. Self-preservation wins out this time.

"Oh, not okay," Nikki says from her vantage point. "The dork with the spiky black hair?"

Spiky hair? I didn't notice any bad hair. "No, the blond." I join Nikki at the door.

Nikki glares for another second, and then her lips twist into a grin. That grin.

Crap.

"Oh, Molls." Her voice is practically a purr.

Double crap. "No."

"Yes." That one word leaves no room for argument. "I'd let him hit on me at work in a heartbeat." No greater sin, unless the guy passes the cuteness test.

I hold up a hand. "No. He made a *Star Trek* reference at me." So what if that isn't exactly the truth. "He's a geek."

"So what?" Nikki says. "You love that stuff. You've been trying to convince me to see the new movie since it came out."

I'm aware of that, but if Nikki thinks I'm going to ask Craig to go …. "Well, I'm not seeing it with him. I repeat. He's a geek, and I don't date geeks."

"Who said anything about dating? It's one night. Make an exception." Nikki's blue eyes sparkle. She grabs my arm and pushes me toward the bar. "Now, get that hunk his drink and get your butt out there, pronto."

I stumble but don't fall. So much for best friend support. What would it cost her to see *Star Trek* with me? We could go at a time when there won't be lots of geeky twenty-somethings. She could be a good friend and not try to get me to go with some guy I don't even know. Never mind that Craig's eyes are that perfect elven green and that he's that sweet spot between buffed and lanky. *Star Trek* reference, mother's basement, video games—everything that lifestyle implies. Good looks are no reason to throw away all the progress I've made on my heartbreak since the last time I didn't let those things bother me.

I mix two of the tranyas and reenter the kitchen to find Nikki where I left her. "Don't you have tables to wait?"

"Just finished checking on them," she says. "It's remarkably dead in here for a Thursday. Your pretty boy and his friends are the biggest group we have."

I groan. "He's not my pretty boy. He's not my anything. What happened to your high horse about getting hit on at work?"

Nikki shakes her head. "You know that only applies to guys who aren't obvious matches. Now, get out there."

Obvious matches? She's been reading too many romance novels since we last had this discussion. Regardless, I can only stand here for so long before the customer decides the delay means bad service. Bad service equals bad tips, and I need the tips. Besides, it's just drinks. "I'm going." I even start walking to prove it.

Two girls—a brunette and a redhead—approach Craig's table.

The brunette has her hair braided, and she runs her fingertips along the back of Craig's neck.

My heart gives one painful thump. "He's taken." Which is a good thing.

"Oh?" Nikki says.

I said that out loud? Oh well. "Yeah, by the brunette. Check out her hand."

"What about it?" Nikki says after a second. "She tapped him on the shoulder."

This time my heart's thump is excited. Stop it. "She caressed his neck."

Nikki gives me a gentle push toward the table. "Nice try, but she's got the friends-since-the-womb aura going on. Don't make me escort you out there and announce that you were too chicken to come alone because you think blondie is hot."

"I'll just drop these off." I start moving. I've known Nikki long enough to know she's not joking.

"And don't forget to talk to him to gage date potential."

"Right." With friends like this, dot … dot … dot.

A third girl joins the pack, and my stomach flips. She's a definite Lara Croft type, if Lara Croft dyed a chunk of her hair purple and found a tattoo artist. The combat boots are just an added bonus. If she's Craig's girlfriend, I'm proceeding with caution.

Lara-deluxe sits and pulls a binder out of her bag. She doesn't move toward him. She doesn't even look at him. It's safe.

"You will not be starting in a tavern." What is she talking about? They are in a tavern.

I set the tranyas down, cutting Lara off mid-sentence. "Three more? What would you ladies like to drink?"

The redhead orders a lemonade. The brunette orders

cranberry juice, and ... Marshalls and Magics?

So that's what Lara pulled out of the binder, full-blown character sheets from the online generator. The badly organized papers my college group used pale by comparison. Craig is playing a wereclaw shifter—oof, ugly—and his class is shaman.

Shaman. Six letters douse my excitement as swift as a glass of ice water down my back. Ward played a shaman. Ward played everything. Nikki can deal. I'm not asking this guy anywhere.

"Water," Lara says. "Neat."

Lemonade, cranberry, water neat. Shaman—no, that's not a drink. "I'll be right back with those." Again, I race back to the kitchen. Not fair. I haven't thought about Ward in months. I moved back home to forget about him, and then a guy shows up at my work with his *Star Trek* quotes and his M and M character sheet. I hate my life.

"Well?" Nikki says the nanosecond I step into the kitchen. "How did it go?"

"Lemonade, cranberry juice, water neat." It's a measure of how out of it I am that it takes me until I reach the bar to realize someone actually ordered water neat.

Nikki shouts something about how bad I am at flirting. I ignore her, at least partly because of water neat. There are lines I just won't cross. Dating gamer guys is one of them. This is what I get for working in a place that serves free tranya and dresses its employees in red shirts when *Star Trek* movies come out.

I deliver the drinks and ask about food. The other guy at the table deliberates over every appetizer for about five minutes, and I bite my lip. Spiky hair is putting it mildly. It looks like the Boy Who Lived survived sticking his finger in an electrical socket. He finally settles on his first choice, wings, and I take the remaining orders. Halfway through his rant, my phone gives five distinct vibrations. Thank the pantheon I remembered to put it on silent. Five buzzes means a notification from Lords of Caldreth, my one guilty geeky pleasure. Ward got me hooked on it. I've tried to stop, but the RPG mechanics are addicting. Besides, no one ever has to know, least of all Craig.

When they finish, I collect menus. "I'll have those right out."

"Thanks," Craig says. His voice is soft and warm.

I grip the menus as if they're my only tether to life. They may be the only thing keeping me from falling into the abyss of want. It's time to put some distance between us. "You're welcome."

Back in the kitchen, I deposit the menus and receive a non-Caldreth set of buzzes from my phone. Putting in the order takes a few minutes, and then I retreat to a corner to check stuff. Caldreth is a quest notification. I tap remind me later and click over to my e-mail. It's from Graphic Art Inc.

I swallow, hard. It's a response to the job application I put in a few weeks ago. Why are they responding at this hour? Is that good? I mean, they wouldn't send a response outside of business hours if it was bad news, would they? Well, they might, but staring at the e-mail isn't going to answer the question. Fingers trembling, I open it and read.

Thank you for your application, but ...

That's all I need. My entire body sags. I needed that job. I need any job that pays better than waitressing. If I'd known my family was going to have this kind of financial troubles after I graduated, I wouldn't have majored in graphic design. Okay, yes I would have. It's not a hopeless industry. It's competitive.

It's just not an earn-money-fast career.

"Molls?" Nikki stops in front of me and gives my phone a pointed glance.

I slide it back into my pocket. "Just checking my mail. I got another no-thanks from a job."

Nikki's eyes soften. She's been listening to my financial issues since my dad got laid off a month ago. "I'm sorry."

I shrug and use the motion to get back into the feel of waitressing. "Me too."

She moves so I can come out of the corner. "Did you at least talk to hottie?"

Like that, my sadness about the job goes away. "No, and I'm not going to. He's just like Ward."

Nikki raises an eyebrow. "You don't even know him."

"I don't have to." And I don't. Geek guys are all alike. They want the hottest new game or the hotter geek girl across the room. Tears start to form. I blink them back. This is exactly why I can't go near Craig. Like Nikki said, I don't even know him, and I'm this upset. I take a deep breath and let it out, slow. "I'm not interested, anyway."

"Okay," Nikki says, doubt in her voice. "I need to check my tables."

That makes two of us, seeing as I don't have the next job lined up and won't be quitting tonight. Until I get out of waitressing, though, it looks like I'm still relying on tip money, which means I'd better follow Nikki's lead and hope my tables like my service enough to leave twenty percent.

Chapter 3: Craig

"The creature gives off disbelieving vibes," Dawn says. "Roll bluff."

Parker does his funky shimmy-dance thing and rolls. "With bonus calculations … I bluff expertly with seventeen."

"That's enough," Dawn says.

"Hah!" Parker shoves his fist in the air. "Take that, creature. That's what you get for messing with Piff the Eviscerator!"

I exchange a look with Lyd. Where did Parker even get that name? He's playing a gnome illusionist mage, and Eviscerator makes no sense. Then again, neither does Parker.

Dawn clears her throat. "So Puff—"

"Piff," Parker says, wounded.

Sonya sings about magical dragons under her breath.

"Silence." Parker grabs his gnome token and holds it up. "Piff the Eviscerator's patience grows tiny."

"Won't take much," Lyd says.

The entire table, minus Parker, collapses into laughter. This is the life. There is no better way to spend a Thursday night.

Well, I could be with Molly. Wow, Craig, chill about the waitress. She probably doesn't even remember you. We spent

14

an hour or so at A's before calling the PDGs—public displays of geekdom—quits and regrouping at my family's house. Where I still live because I have another year of broke college student-dom. Broke-ness didn't stop me from tipping twenty-five percent, though, and I can't bring myself to regret the decision. I'm hooked.

Or desperate. Happens when there's been no one for over a year.

"Moving on." Dawn taps the grid matt on which she drew a rough map. "The creature steps aside and allows you to pass. You walk for another hour and then find yourself at the closed gates of a city. An elf sits off to one side."

Parker moves his piece beside Lyd's. "'Hale, traveler. I am Piff the Eviscerator.' I brandish my staff. 'Why do you sit outside this city?'"

"'Because the gates are closed,'" Lyd says, deadpan.

"'Well, yes.'" Parker is not deterred. "'But why this particular city?'"

"'It was the only one nearby.'"

I cover my mouth to hide my smile. Lyd's master smart-ass skills strike again.

"'Why do you not give me a straight answer, elf?'"

"'Kobri,'" Lyd says. "'And because you're short.'"

Sonya bursts out laughing.

Parker's face turns beat red. "I will not be mocked!" It's impossible to tell if that's him or Piff talking.

"'Too bad,'" Lyd says in character. She grins and holds her hand up to me.

I slap a high five and join Sonya in laughing. We're loud enough to wake the undead, which is why I put us in the den and not in the living room. The latter has no door.

15

Speaking of the door, someone knocks.

I clear my throat and get myself under control. "Come in."

My mom does just that. She's wearing a black dress and four-inch heels. Her hair is up, and diamonds or something similar glint at her throat and ears. "You kids having fun?"

Kids? It sounds like we're twelve. Granted, we're acting like it, but still.

"Evening, Mrs. Lawrence," Lyd says. "We are."

Mom flashes a grin. "Cathy to you all, you know that." She winks.

I stand. "Headed out?" It's a stupid question considering Mom's outfit.

She nods. "There's a great new *place* opening up downtown."

My throat tightens as if I've swallowed a mouthful of dust. The emphasis on the word *place* leaves no question that she means bar. Not that there's anything wrong with that. My folks aren't dead, but they're supposed to be waiting for my sister to get home. "What about Amber?"

Mom waves a hand. "She should be home by ten thirty, but your father and I need to get going. If you could keep an ear for her, honey."

What? This was not part of the agreement. I'm busy. Mom acknowledged my room full of friends. She knows we're playing a game. "I—"

"Thank you, Craig." Mom gives me a hug. Under her perfume is the slight scent of rum. Wonderful, she'll be shattered by the time she gets home.

"Is Dad sober?" I can't help it. The question just comes out.

She steps back. "Of course." Translation, *probably*. "Anyway, we're off. See you kids later."

The kids chorus a *goodbye*.

I follow Mom into the hall and to the door. A far-too-fancy light fixture hangs over the foyer, and the wooden stairs to the second floor empty into the entryway. Dad's beside the front door, Mom's jacket over one arm. He helps her into it and runs his hands down her sides.

I ignore the implications behind that. I don't want the images. "When will you guys be back, do you think?"

"Later," Dad says. "Don't burn the place down." He laughs.

I don't. "Have fun." My voice is bitter.

"We will," Mom says. With that, they take their leave.

I stare at the door and wait for the roaring in my ears to subside. Just once, it would be nice if they remembered that they have a fifteen-year-old daughter and that I'm not said fifteen-year-old's father. I lost my last girlfriend because they couldn't keep that in mind, and I now have to pause my evening to keep an eye out for my sister. I glance at my watch. Whose curfew is in ten minutes. The hell? My folks couldn't wait ten more minutes?

I trudge back down the hall before I decide punching something is a good idea. I'm going to have to talk to them, again.

"Everything okay?" Lyd says when I get back. Her tone holds the frustration I'm trying to keep at bay.

I shrug and flop into my chair. "As okay as it can be. I need to wait for Amber."

Dawn nods. "We can take a break. We've gotten two of you to the city."

Parker stands. "To the living room." He leads the parade out of the den.

Lyd falls into step beside me when we're in the hall. "I'm sorry."

17

I shrug. What is there to say? This has been life since Amber went through puberty two years ago. At least then my folks were on board with parenting. "She'll be home in about five minutes. Then we can get back to the game." I sit on the living room couch.

Lyd sits next to me, and the rest take the matching pleather chairs. The glass-top coffee table at the room's center holds the remote, but no one reaches for it. No one even moves.

"Who cast the stasis spell?" I say.

Possible responses are cut off by a car door shutting outside. That was fast. If I'd known, I wouldn't have dragged everyone out here.

The door opens and closes, and Amber comes into view. She's wearing a miniskirt, a belly shirt, and at least four-inch heels.

The living room disappears. Before I can stop myself, I'm up and moving. Something holds me back, but I tug free. Hell, no. "You did not go out dressed like that."

My sister sweeps toward the stairs.

"Hello?" I close the distance in three strides, grab her arm, and spin her to face me. "Answer the question."

She glares at me through her fake eyelashes. Where did she get fake eyelashes? "Hi, not-mom."

"I don't care who I'm not." I can feel my blood pressure rising. "My fifteen-year-old sister did not go out looking like some cheap gun-toting hooker."

Amber pulls out of my grip. "Yeah, I did, and gun-toting hookers aren't cheap, just FYI."

I don't want to know how she knows that. Clearly, though, the big-brother approach isn't working. I put my hands up, palms out. When I talk, my voice is calmer. "Look, Amber, I just don't want you to get hurt—"

"Or taken advantage of." She plants her hands on her hips. "Well, brother mine, you aren't my father, so no matter how many times you tell me that, I don't have to listen." She punctuates the statement by stomping up the steps. Her footfalls pound overhead, and then a second door, this one to her room, slams.

Quiet descends on the foyer, my ragged breathing the only sound. Holy crap. This cannot go on. I cannot have a heart attack at age twenty-one. If Amber keeps coming home dressed like that, though, it's a definite possibility.

"Craig?" Lyd rests a hand on my shoulder.

I inhale and let the breath out, slow. "I'm okay." There's nothing I can do right this second. No use getting worked up over it. I'll talk to Mom and Dad, which will hopefully do something useful.

"Well, that was interesting," Sonya says in a disapproving tone.

It sure was. I shake my head. I need something to get my mood back on track. Mood ... food. Here's to rhyming! "We should eat." My excitement dies as I realize I have no snacks in the house. "Which will require a trip to the store."

"To the nearest establishment that sells sustenance without health benefits," Parker says as if announcing a sports game.

"That works." I pull my keys off the hook by the door. "Can I trust you three in my house for a half hour?"

"Is the Pope Jewish?" Lyd says, wandering back into the living room.

Right. Shop fast. "Let's go." I go outside. The night air is cool, compliments of June in New England. Parker and I pile into my car, and we're off.

The ride is uneventful. Parker babbles about Piff the Eviscerator's many talents. I keep my eyes on the road and try not to think about my baby sister getting taken advantage of. Where did she even get clothes like that? Not that clothing makes a difference, but some guy's going to take that as an invitation, and he's not going to care. And so much for calming down. I breathe again and start actually listening to Parker. It's a sad day when listening to the accomplishments of a gnome named Piff the Eviscerator, who doesn't eviscerate anything, is calming.

"So," Parker says when we arrive at the store. "What is it our mission to obtain?"

I beep the car locked and jog across the lot. "Anything but Fig Newtons." I swallow the nasty phantom taste. Lyd brought them last time. Ugh. "I don't care what Madam Elf wants."

We enter the store, and Parker grabs a basket. "Let the search commence." He salutes and promenades—there's no other word for it—away.

I get my own basket and saunter in the opposite direction. Food shopping for M and M is all about carbs and caffeine. I pass the cleaning supplies aisle—useless—and skirt a family of five with two toddlers. What are families of five with toddlers even doing here at this hour? A voice comes over the staticky loudspeaker and garbles some message that is completely indiscernible to anyone who speaks whatever language that is. I pick up my pace. Anything but Fig Newtons and get out. Next time we need midnight snacks, I hit a smaller store.

A group of teens flail toward me in typical we-are-seventeen-and-exploring-what-it's-like-to-drive-ourselves-places fashion. Why can't Amber be like them? No, I have to have the type of sibling who rebels by trying to act twenty-five. Slice me in half with a lightsaber.

I play a quick game of dodgem and turn down the next aisle—cereal. This works. Brightly colored packages wink at me from the shelves—crunch, sugar, rainbow taste. It's not till I get past the silly rabbit that I strike gold. A's isn't the only place celebrating *Star Trek*. Captain Spock gives me a stoic stare from the front of a box.

I get caught in the tractor beam—thanks, Scottie. Somewhere in the back of my mind, I know it's just regular cereal that's shaped differently so the manufacturer can charge an extra dollar, but the tractor beam's having none of it. I reach for the box. It's in my hand. It's mine.

"Excuse me."

What the ...? I jump and spin, nearly dropping the coveted box.

A blonde girl about my age, is leaning against the shelves. She's familiar somehow, but I can't place her.

"Sorry," I say.

She checks something on her phone and shakes her head. "No problem. I actually have a potentially awkward question. You probably don't recognize me, but I work at A's. I was there when you were earlier. My friend, your waitress, wanted to ask if you're interested in seeing the new *Star Trek* movie tomorrow night, but she didn't get a chance."

For a second, it's like she's speaking Klingon. I have to actually let the words process. My waitress at A's—Molly—wants to see the *Star Trek* movie tomorrow. I replay the gist of the speech. That sounds right, but it can't be. If Molly was interested, she would have talked to me, not given me the you're-such-a-geek stare.

"You breathing?" the blonde says.

"Uh." Yup, and incapable of English too. "Let me get this straight. Your friend wants to see *Star Trek* with me?"

She points to the cereal. "I can't imagine you aren't interested in the movie."

She's got me there. I've been waiting for this movie, and I've been anticipating going alone. No one in the group is into *Star Trek* like I am. Here's a chance to go with someone and not just anyone, Molly, who I want to see again anyway.

"Sure." Talk about a golden opportunity.

"Awesome, I'll tell her. Do you have a phone number or something?"

I give it, and she puts it into her phone.

"Cool." She puts her phone away and holds out her hand. "Her name is Molly, and I'm Nikki, by the way."

I shake her hand and bite down before I make myself look like a weirdo by saying something poetic like armies of angry bugbears couldn't have made me forget Molly's name. "Nice to meet you."

"Likewise," Nikki says. "Have fun tomorrow night." She gives me a little wave and strolls away.

I stare after her until she's out of sight. Then I stare at Spock. "I can't believe that just happened."

Predictably, Spock remains silent. Even so, his response is clear. *Fascinating. But it did happen.* Spock is never wrong.

I make sure no one is around and then skip down the aisle. I have a date with Molly!

Chapter 4: Molly

Twenty-five percent. Craig tipped me twenty-five percent … in cash. That's five percent more than standard. And he didn't leave his number, which means he's not expecting anything in return.

I tuck the tip into my pocket and stroll back to the kitchen. The last two hours of my shift are going to be murder. Ten till midnight on a Thursday—it's going to be all college students, which I don't mind when I'm one of them. But serving them …? Just, no.

"You're looking awful happy," Nikki says as I pass her. "Did a certain blond hunk leave you some digits?"

I start to tell her about the extra tip but clamp my mouth closed. It will only empower her. Besides, I shouldn't be blushing like some preteen over a guy I don't ever want to know beyond customer/server. He's a geek.

That does it. I stiffen. "No. I'm just glad him and his friends are gone. They were loud."

Nikki shrugs. "Well, it's going to get a lot louder. The bar's about to fill up."

I turn and bite my lip to keep from screaming. A troop of college kids settle onto stools at one end of the bar, and they're all dressed for a place much more risqué than this.

"Pregamers," I say.

"And seasoned ones." Nikki points to one of the girls. "Check that one out."

I do. She's got long dark hair, an expanse of skin showing on the top half of her body, and two guys practically on top of her. "Wonderful."

"Isn't it just?" Nikki pats my shoulder. "Fortunately for me and unfortunately for you, my shift is over." She blows me a kiss and dashes for the building's rear exit.

I glare after her. She's lucky she's my friend.

As predicted, the next two hours are a nightmare. The one bright spot is a text from Nikki at eleven thirty telling me we have plans for tomorrow night. That's something to look forward to while I try to not die at work. At one point, one of the waiters and I almost serve the same people two different orders. It's a good thing we're good at our jobs. Not that being good makes it any easier. It's a mess either way, and at eleven fifty-nine, I'm in the kitchen, tapping my nails on the wall and watching the clock. Change, change, change …

Midnight.

Thank the pantheon.

And there I go with the geeky thoughts again. A guy who was playing Marshalls and Magics—as a shaman, don't forget—left you a twenty-five percent tip when he didn't need to. That's all there is to it. Stop letting the inner geek out of the closet.

I punch out and make my exit. Desdemona—my car which I gave a Shakespeare-inspired name—shines a silvery black in the half moon's light. I get in and start her up. My phone buzzes while I'm backing out of the spot. It's Mom, which is weird. She never calls this late when she knows I'm at work. I tap to answer. "Hi, Mom."

"Hi, honey." She's in a cheery mood. "Are you still at work?" And she wants something.

I take my foot off the gas. Driving and talking on the phone do not mix. "I just got out. What's up?"

"Can you stop at the store and pick up some stuff?"

My stomach clenches. The emphasis she puts on *store* makes it clear she wants me to go somewhere that doesn't cost a lot, namely because we can't afford it. "Yeah, what do you need?"

She gives me a list, which contains several types of prepared meals. I hang up and resume driving, hooking a left, instead of a right, out of the lot. So much for going straight home and collapsing on my bed.

A few minutes later, I cruise into the local low-priced grocery store's lot. It's almost full. Why the place is always teeming with people at midnight, I'll never know, and I'll definitely never like it. At least I'm a seasoned shopper. I get everything on the list and conduct a perimeter search of the rest of the store for items of interest. I pass the cereal aisle and freeze. There's a box with Spock on it. I shouldn't. I don't need it, but it's Spock, and Spock wins.

"I had a feeling you'd buy that."

I leap about a thousand parsecs. That voice sounds like Nikki, but it can't be her. She never shops here.

Despite that, she's strolling down the aisle toward me with a twelve-pack of toilet paper.

I hesitate with the cereal half off the shelf. "What are you doing here?"

"Shopping," she says. Thank you, Lady Obvious. "I was headed toward checkout when I saw you come in. Then you ran through the store like Godzilla was chasing you."

My cheeks warm. "Sorry about that. I'm—"

"Not fond of this place. I know." She points to my cart. "Are you going to put the cereal in there?"

I tighten my grip on the box. She's already seen me holding it. It's not like I can just let go and keep walking, pretending I'm not interested. A quick survey of the aisle reveals no other shoppers. I toss the box in my carriage and start toward the front of the store. It's just one splurge, and on my checking account be it.

"So," I say when we reach the end of the aisle. "How's your free time since leaving A's been?"

"Freeing," she says, falling into step beside me. "How was A's?"

I wave a hand. "Not freeing in the slightest." It's a sign of how true it is that there's no argument. I seriously need a new job. "But you probably guessed that. What are these plans for tomorrow, by the way?"

Nikki slips in front of me and gets into line. "We're meeting a friend of mine for dinner."

Dinner? Great. Doesn't she remember my financial issues? Eating out isn't really in the budget. "Oh."

"Don't sound so happy," she says without turning around. "It will be fun. Promise."

Sure it will, just not for the previously mentioned checking account. I lean back on my heels and wait. The woman in front of Nikki goes through her five million coupons, which takes about fifty million years. Despite this, Nikki doesn't go to another line, and I'm too tired to bother.

An eon or so later, Nikki pays for her toilet paper. I follow suit, swiping my card and wincing at the thirty-dollar detract. There goes my tip. If it wouldn't be beyond embarrassing,

I'd feel obligated to figure out where Craig lives and send him a thank-you. As it is, I'll have to content myself with the knowledge that he paid for my family's food. I retrieve my bags and follow Nikki out of the store. The temperature goes up twenty degrees from the store to outside, and I let out a residual shiver.

"I'll pick you up tomorrow," Nikki says, stopping beside Dessy. "Not sure what time yet."

I pop the trunk and shove my stuff inside. "Text me."

"Will do. Have a good night." She wanders away.

"You too." I close the trunk and deliver my carriage to the nearest return thingy. Then I get in, start Dessy, and head home. Ten minutes later, I pull into my driveway and haul the bags into the house.

Mom is in the living room watching some soap opera. She gives me a little wave when I enter. I nod back and lug the stuff to the kitchen. If I move fast I can have everything away before a commercial break. I'm just shoving the last box in the freezer when Mom strolls into the room. Foiled again.

"How was work?" She leans against the counter.

I stall by gathering the plastic bags and stuffing them in the bottom drawer beside the fridge. "Fine."

She nods. "Any news?"

And here ends the stalling. I've been collecting job rejections for the last month. Dad or I need to get a job, fast. The savings is only going to last so long, and Mom's work just doesn't pay enough.

"I got another rejection."

Mom blinks and looks away. She's going to cry. I can't handle it when she cries.

"Well," she says, her voice a little shaky. "You know what

27

they say. Every no brings you closer to a yes." It's her standard response whenever I don't get a job, and while she means well, it doesn't help.

"I still have a few applications out." What I don't say is that I don't know what I'll do if those don't work—maybe be forced to apply for secretarial jobs, but I'm not ready to consider that just yet. Graphic design only has so many career options. I mean, I could freelance, but that's not reliable enough.

Mom shrugs and straightens. A deep breath brings the forced smile back to her face. Somehow, she's always able to stand up and face life, even when it sucks. "Well, we'll just wait for the next one." She pats my shoulder. "Why don't you go get some rest. I'm sure you're exhausted."

As if saying it makes it true, I yawn. I am tired, but there's more to it than that. *You're tired* is mom's cue that she wants to be alone, which is fine. I kind of need some me-time too.

I give her a quick hug. "I'll see you in the morning."

She kisses my forehead. "Night, sweetie."

We go back into the living room. She settles on the couch, and I go upstairs. In my room, I close the door and flop on my Justice League comforter. It's something else I couldn't bring myself to get rid of. I bury my face in my pillows. Maybe I should have asked Craig out. I can't get a better job. I can't stand A's anymore. I can't watch my mom be this stressed out anymore. What would a date with a geek be compared to all that?

Chapter 5: Craig

Where the hell is Parker? Seriously, the kid needs a keeper. I've been wandering around the store for ten minutes, and he's nowhere to be found. Never mind that I have to remind myself not to start skipping every few steps. Nikki might still be in the store, and if she catches me prancing like one of Santa's reindeer, that date she just set me up for is history.

"Ahoy, light-haired shifter friend!" Parker shouts from about twenty feet away.

Or maybe Parker is going to kill that date for me. At least I know where he is. I take my three items and ditch my basket. We can combine for a faster checkout.

Parker closes the distance, and all plans about getting out of here quickly die a short and painful death. His basket is practically overflowing. How did he get all that in such a short time?

I stop in front of him and hold on to my stuff. It's not like there's room for it anyway. "What the hell are you buying?"

He grabs a package of gummy bears and holds it up as if it's the dragon's treasure. "We shall consume tiny gummy creatures."

All those are gummy bears? I reverse directions and make a beeline for the registers. The M and M gods better be listening if Piff wants to survive the night. "You're a tiny gummy creature."

"Gnomes can be gummy," Parker says, matching my stride.

"I don't want to know." I get in the shortest line available—one person ahead of me—and toss my stuff on the belt.

Parker upends his basket, and gummy bear packages fly everywhere. "Oops."

I pick up a bunch of the ones closest to me and slide them onto the bottom of a nearby display shelf. Five M and M'ers can only eat so many gummy bears, especially when at least one—Lyd—doesn't even like them. We pay—me significantly less than Parker—and exit the store with about thirty people watching us. At least none of them are Nikki.

The ride back is filled with Parker talking about Piff some more, and we arrive at my house a little after twelve thirty. I grab my one bag and leave him to unload his five.

"We're back," I say, rather unnecessarily, when I open the front door.

The girls wander out of the living room, talking and laughing. There's no sign of Amber, which is either very good or very bad.

"Everything's all right, right?" I say. It's a stupid question given the girls' calm attitudes, but the twitching in my chest won't go away until I'm sure.

"Quiet as a seclusion chamber with an unconscious occupant," Sonya says.

That takes my straightforward-answer-wanting brain a minute to process. "All's well, then. Good."

"Yes," Lyd says, bumping my shoulder with hers. "Now, what

took you so long? Were you building an establishment that sells unhealthy snacks?"

Parker takes that moment to squeeze his way through the doorway. "Silence, elf." He marches down the hall. "Follow."

The girls give me questioning glances.

I shrug, close the door, and start after our gnome. What do they want me to say? They'll find out soon enough anyway.

"Behold," Parker says when we're all in the den. He upends the bag of gummy bears. They don't fly everywhere this time. Pity. "We bring fair nourishment."

Sonya rolls her eyes. "Gummy bears?"

"Yes." Parker holds up one of the packages and beams. He tosses it back on the table, and the radiant smile turns to a confused frown. "Weren't there more of these?"

"So," I say, sitting. "Whose turn is it?"

Lyd snorts.

"I believe it's yours, Shifter." Dawn takes her seat, not batting an eye. How does she never react to our foolishness? "Prepare yourself. You begin momentarily."

Parker tears open a bag of gummies and shoves a handful in his mouth. "But fir-mm-mm we fea-mm-mm."

"Eloquent," Sonya says, grabbing her own pack and sitting.

"Isn't he just," I say, opening my cereal. No bowl, no spoon, because eating cereal out of the box is how all the cool kids do it. That and I forgot to grab a bowl and spoon when I passed the kitchen, and my turn at show-offery has been put off long enough.

"Are you ready?" Dawn says and bites the head off a gummy bear.

I push the cereal box aside and lean forward. *Do your worst* springs to mind as a response, but I think better of it. With my luck—and Dawn's sick idea of fun—I'd end up fighting a tarrasque. "I was born ready." That's as bad as *do your worst*.

Dawn swallows the poor gummy bear's head. "Then, let us begin. You do, in fact, begin in a tavern. Shifters are common in these parts, and you have accompanied a long-time acquaintance, but not friend, for drinks. And perhaps to make certain this acquaintance does not get so drunk he tries to burn down the city."

I give Parker a pointed look.

He shoves another fistful of gummy bears in his mouth.

"An attractive human bartender approaches you. She gives your acquaintance his fourth drink and leans across the bar."

My mind conjures Molly. Of course.

"'Well, aren't you the dangerous-looking one,'" Dawn says in a terrible flirty voice. At least it makes the picture of Molly shatter. "She waits for a response."

Which she'll get, because I can concentrate much better without Molly on the brain. "I take a swig of my half-full drink and set the glass back down. 'So they tell me.'"

"The waitress twirls a clump of hair around one finger and gazes at you through long eyelashes. 'Wanna prove it?'"

Hell yeah. This is why I didn't get a bowl and spoon. "'How?'"

Dawn flips a page in her binder. "'Word from some new-comers is there's a gnome causing trouble outside the east gate. Shooting off colorful magic.'"

Parker pauses in his epic quest to eat fifteen gummy bears at once. "Piff—mm mm—e –viserat—mm does—mm—"

"Really, dude?" Sonya whaps his shoulder. "Yes, you do cause that kind of mischief, and talking with a mouth full of gummy bears is gross."

Parker scowls.

"'Is that so?'" I say before he can start talking again.

"The waitress nods. 'My daddy's a prominent figure here, and he doesn't much like gnomes. I bet he'd be grateful if someone eliminated the little thing.' She bats her eyes. 'I know I would.'"

Admiral Ackbar appears in my head and shouts something about this being a trap. He's right, but I'm going to follow in my predecessors' footsteps and not listen. "'I suppose I could assist.'" And as if my impending doom isn't bad enough, the image of Molly is coming back. I must be more excited about tomorrow than I thought.

Tomorrow, crap.

"Craig?" Lyd waves a hand in my face. "You paying attention?"

I blink out of a stupor. I forgot all about our session tomorrow night. Not that I'm gonna cancel on Molly. I've waited too long for a real date. The xp dent is going to burn, but I'll deal with it. We're only first level.

I hold up three fingers, our signal for pause. "Before I forget, I won't be able to make it tomorrow night."

"Oh?" Lyd says, raising an eyebrow. "Hot date?"

For some reason, that stings. I know it's a joke, but is the idea of me going on a date really that far-fetched? "Actually, yeah, with our waitress from A's. We're going to see *Star Trek*."

"Whoop!" Parker claps me on the back, hard. Good thing I didn't have a mouthful of food. "That is excellent news, and we must feast." He grabs another bunch of bears.

Sonya grabs his wrist before he can get them to his mouth. "Do not try and talk while eating those." She releases him and faces me. "'Grats, Craig, that's great news. You learned how to talk to her, after all."

"Yeah," Lyd says, less enthusiastic. She almost sounds upset, but then she yawns. Just tired, then. "Have fun."

"Thanks." The goofy grin from the store threatens to return, and I cover it by reaching for more cereal. "K, back in game. 'I'll go have a look for this gnome.' My character departs the tavern, leaving the potentially dangerous friend at the bar, and makes his way toward the east gate. 'Excuse me, guard, I was asked to check out trouble beyond the city wall.'"

"The guard grunts and opens the gate just wide enough for you to pass. 'Go. But you gotta stay out there till morning.'" Dawn's thug impression is way better than her flirty one.

I finish chewing and swallow before talking. A novel concept at this table. "'Fine.' I go through the gate."

"The gate closes with a clang behind you," Dawn says. "It is dark, but the moon gives you enough light to see a tree ahead. You may hear voices. Roll perception."

Here we are, the moment of truth. I grab my D20 and let it fall.

Two.

I slap my forehead. "Eleven total."

"You may hear voices," Dawn says.

How informative. "Is there anything else I can roll to help?"

Dawn shrugs one shoulder. "Insight, perhaps."

I can take a hint. I roll and get a three. "Twelve." Apparently this isn't my night. So much for show-offery. May as well just approach the voices at this point.

"I suggest you approach the voices," Dawn says. Great minds.

I move my token toward Parker's and Lyd's. "I'll approach the voices." And hope my date goes better than my rolls.

Chapter 6: Molly

J eans and a nice shirt—good enough. I brush my hair and swipe on some lip gloss. Nikki's friend better be a nice person. If they aren't, this night is not going to be worth it, and where we're eating out, I need to get my money's worth.

I toss my hairbrush back onto my dresser and sit on the edge of my bed. The light-blue walls of my room give off a calming aura, the benefit of cool colors. The hardwood floors and dark furniture make it look like any twenty-something's room. Really, it's only the comforter that's weird, and I'm allowed that one guilty pleasure.

My phone buzzes. A text from Nikki pops up. *Out front.* As usual, she's ridiculously on time. She said five thirty. It's exactly five thirty.

I text that I'm coming and grab my purse. Time to get this over with. The walk down the stairs and through the living room is a death march, and the click of the door opening is the guard locking the cell and tossing the key.

Nikki is standing on the porch, and she's wearing a dress. Why is she wearing a dress?

But I don't have time to ask. She takes one look at me and barges inside. "You are not wearing that."

"Why?" I try to push her back outside, but she's determined and stronger than me. "What's wrong with it?"

"What's wrong with it?" She asks the question as if she's beseeching strength. "We're going out to dinner at a restaurant that isn't A's. That's what's wrong with it."

I grip the corner of the wall for leverage. It doesn't help. I'm swept along with the tide. "For your information, I'm way overdressed for A's. And where exactly are we going? You know I can't afford anything too fancy."

"It's not too fancy." Nikki practically hauls me up the stairs. "It's just a Friday night, and you can do better than jeans."

I stumble into my room and turn the light back on.

She yanks my closet open and starts moving hangers. "I know you have something." She pauses at the Jedi robe I bought for a convention a few years ago and shakes her head.

I let that pass. "Really, I look fine. It's not like I'm wearing a T-shirt—"

"Shush." She points to the bed. "Sit. Wait." There's no arguing with her tone.

So I sit. "Yes, ma'am."

Nikki ignores me and continues rifling through my closet. She passes a yellow and blue sundress and a green jacket before stopping at a black flowy skirt. "Perfect." She pulls it out and tosses it at me. "Hold on to that. Now, what do you have for shirts?" She shoves all the hangers back to their original positions and just stares for a minute. "Nothing. What else do you have?"

I hold up the skirt. Where are we going that this is necessary? And what kind of shirt do I need to go with this? Not that the skirt is overly fancy, but it's more than I bargained for.

"Molls?" Nikki taps my shoulder. "You need an outfit today."

I scowl. "I'm thinking." So what if I'm really not. Is it too late to back out of this? God, I'm a terrible friend for even thinking it. It's one night, and I can find a shirt to go with the flowy skirt.

Flowy, that's it. I snap my fingers, because that's how the cool kids acknowledge good ideas, and cross to the dresser. I force open the bottom drawer and sift through the shirts crammed within. Of course it's at the bottom, but at least it isn't wrinkled. Victory. I yank out the red flowy top.

"Perfect," Nikki says, backing into the hall. "Get changed." She pulls the door closed.

I glare at the closed door. Nikki's a single-woman army when she wants to be. I get changed and kick off my loafers, which are no longer suitable. Instead, I bottom off, because top off makes no sense when talking about shoes, with a pair of strappy black sandals. Just in case, I dawn silver stud earrings and add blush and eye shadow to my ensemble. I've gone this far. Why stop now?

"Much better," Nikki says when I open the door. "Let's move. We're going to be late." She kills my bedroom light and leads the way downstairs and out to her car.

"I still don't see why I couldn't meet you there," I say, getting into the front passenger side. "I drive too."

Nikki gets in and starts the engine. "Because we're saving the environment. Buckle up."

Saving the environment? Right. I click my seat belt into place, and we start moving. "So where are we going again?"

"An inexpensive restaurant." Nikki navigates to the end of my street and onto the main drag. "Don't worry. I've got your best interests in mind."

Why does that terrify me? I settle into the seat and watch

the quaint homes of my neighborhood pass. "If you say so."

She pats my arm when she stops at the next intersection. "Trust me."

The drive is uneventful and quiet. A few turns later, Nikki pulls into the mall parking lot.

Every hair on my body stands on edge. Why are we going to the mall on a Friday night? It's going to be swarming with high school kids. "This restaurant is at the mall?"

"Sort of," Nikki says.

What does *sort of* mean? It's either at the mall or it isn't. Something's wrong here. "Nikki, what's going on?"

She pulls into a parking spot in front of the movie theater. She gazes out her window for a minute before nodding and facing me. "Our friend is here." She points.

Since when is it our friend, but whatever. I look where she's pointing, and my insides light on fire.

The person we're meeting is Craig.

"Huh?" It can't be. This has to be a joke or a mistake or something. Why would we be meeting Craig? She said we were meeting a friend of hers. She didn't recognize him yesterday at A's, unless that was an act, which makes no sense. "You know him?"

"No," Nikki says. "But you're going to. You're getting dinner and then seeing *Star Trek*."

That fire is going to come out of my mouth in about thirty seconds, and I'm going to feed her to Dr. Evil's mutated sea bass. "You set me up?" I whirl, the low ceiling the only thing keeping me from flailing my arms. "How could you? I told you. Not him. No geeks."

Nikki doesn't so much as blink. "He's waiting."

I fold my arms. "Good for him. He's going to be doing that

for a while."

"Okay." She sits back in her seat. "I don't have anywhere else to go."

Oh no. No way is she doing this to me. "Nikki—"

"Molls." She reaches for my arm.

I pull away.

She puts her hands up as if she'd intended to do that all along. "Seriously, you can't keep running from this. You're a geek. Ward was one jerk—"

"It wasn't just Ward." I could go on for hours about every geek I ever dated—the midnight releases they ditched me for, the complaints when my cosplay wasn't sexy enough, the birthday presents of tickets to something he wanted to go to.

"I know, but not all guys are like that. Not all geeks are like that, and what makes you think that just because a guy isn't a geek, he's nice?"

I freeze, mouth open. I have no answer. There is no unspoken rule that all geeks are jerks, and there's no rule that all non-geeks are nice. For all I know, Craig is an awesome person, but my pride won't let me admit that in front of Nikki.

"I just can't believe you set this up behind my back."

Nikki unlocks the car. "Go have fun. You won't regret it. You can call me to pick you up, unless you find another ride home." She winks.

I open the door. I don't do one-night anythings, and she knows it. "This is not over. We will talk about this later."

"Yeah, yeah." She waves a hand. "Go be yourself."

Clearly, she means my less pissed-off self. I get out of the car and slam the door. I'm barely three steps away before Nikki backs out of the spot and drives away, leaving me officially trapped. Forget the bass, she's getting the laser-beam-enhanced sharks.

I straighten my skirt, mutter a few choice words, and start across the lot. The sky is approaching dark blue, and the lights from the streetlamps and the mall make the parking lot almost as bright as day. Craig leans against the building, looking way too good in black pants and a green shirt. Green shirt—wonderful. We can be the Christmas tree duet, and it's all Nikki's fault. Two more steps see me at the sidewalk. The second I'm on the curb, the fire in my chest dies. As if leaving the relative safety of where I can get run over by a car drains my energy, the anger is gone, replaced by knocking knees and a fluttery stomach. Get a grip. This is not okay. Your best friend set you up with a geek, and despite her logic, geeks have led to nothing but broken hearts and bad movie marathons in the past. There is no place for girly feels here.

Nevertheless, the girly feelings stay. I'm screwed, but there's very little I can do about it now. Get through the night and get this over with. Then I never have to see him again. One night won't kill me. I start toward him.

He detaches from the wall and meets me halfway. "Hey." His voice is soft and warm, just like it was last night.

No, focus. You are not liking this guy. He's a geek. Geek, bad. Normal, good. K, Tarzan? "Hey." Ugh, my voice is soft too.

Fortunately or unfortunately, that's it for the immediate conversation. Craig gives me the once-over. Really, he's a guy. What did I expect? When he's done, he meets my gaze. He doesn't stare at my breasts. Maybe this won't be terrible.

"Red shirt," he says. "Wish I'd thought of it."

Oh hell. I stare at the ground in an effort to hide the blush climbing my cheeks. This is all Nikki's fault. I'm not sure how since she didn't even know the significance between red shirts and *Star Trek until A's made us wear red shirts,* but blaming her helps. Either way, this is bad. I may as well tattoo *massive geek* across my forehead. It would be less obvious. And the worst part is this isn't even planned. I look like a total Trekker nerd without even trying.

"I didn't really think about the color of my shirt." I sound like Minnie Mouse on steroids.

He smiles, and the dimple comes out. "Me neither, but at least your lack of thought put you in style for the movie." Wow, he's got a decent sense of humor, and he's not disappointed that I didn't plan my shirt color.

"I'm not sure a red shirt is the best style for this movie, but …."

He laughs and faces the theater. "So the next showing is at seven fifteen, which gives us plenty of time for food. Do you want Italian or Chinese?" He flails his hand in the general direction of the mall. "Or some other option that I'm not aware of because I haven't been into the actual mall in about five thousand years, and I don't know if they've added more restaurants?"

He didn't even mention the food court. Ward would have dragged me straight there with the excuse that he was saving up for a new game release. Things are really looking up, and if all else fails, it appears we have stuff in common other than *Star Trek.* Though, I'm not sure avoidance of malls is something to base any type of relationship on. "I don't think they have, but I haven't been in there in about five thousand years either. Why don't we go with Italian, and then if something else presents itself, we can go from there?"

"I approve of this plan." Craig starts toward the theater doors.

41

"Though, you're brave. Italian has sauce."

Sauce. I forgot about sauce. I'm not in the mood for Chinese, though, so oh well. "Well, as you pointed out earlier, I am wearing a red shirt."

His eyes go wide. "You wore that because of sauce?" Then he smacks his forehead. "No, you didn't, and I sound like an idiot. Never mind."

I can't help it. I laugh a little. He's kind of cute when he's flustered, which I'm not caring about.

We battle through the people milling around outside but make it to the entrance. Craig holds the door, freaking holds the door. I enter and step to one side while he continues to hold it for the four families that pile in behind me.

"Yikes," he says when he escapes doorstop duty.

"Yeah," I say, and we begin our journey across the labyrinth that is the Freedom Tree Mall movie theater. This is no small feat on a weekend evening. Not only are there more families, there are other couples on dates and, worst of all, groups of tween girls. The latter are everywhere, and they don't care whose way they're standing in. A cluster of what seems like fifty thousand takes up half the width of the theater at one point. They're all vying for a spot in front of a picture of the latest early twenty-something heartthrob that I couldn't name if my life depended on it.

But I needn't worry. Craig, it turns out, is a crowd navigator of the first order. He dodges them without so much as a scratch. All I have to do is follow. That's pretty impressive, and we reach the mall proper unharmed.

"Mission nearly impossible accomplished," he says, hooking a right. "And now that song's gonna be stuck in my head."

Oh good, I'm not the only one. "Nice job back there."

He blushes a little, which is kind of adorable. "I'd say it's a natural talent, but I think credit goes to my hours of misspent time playing video games. Hand-eye coordination and such."

"Oh," I say. "What kinds of games do you play?" Cheese on a moldy cracker, what is wrong with me? I just asked a gamer what he likes to play. I'm never going to learn.

"RPGs mostly." He goes around a mom with a double stroller and then moves back to my side. "Some FPSs. I prefer the type where I have to get to know my character, but I'm a twenty-something guy. Sometimes I just wanna shoot things."

I try not to stare at him, partly because not watching where I'm going is dangerous in this mall. That's it? No list of games I've never heard of? No in-depth analysis of the difference between gameplay styles? No ranting about best scores? "I ... know that feeling." That feels very unfinished. "The shooting things part, I mean. I get it at work a lot."

He opens and holds the door to the Italian restaurant, Allegro's. Seriously, he was raised in the eighteen hundreds. "Joys of waitressing?"

I enter ahead of him and wait for him to follow. "Let's just say the bar can get a little interesting."

"Two?" the host says. Unlike my place of employment, these people know how to dress their employees—white shirt and black pants. But then, this place makes A's look like a topless bar. Craig affirms that there are, in fact, two of us, and the host gathers the appropriate number of menus and place settings.

"*Me seguire*," he says and walks away.

"I think that's follow," I say.

"Safe bet since they haven't brought out the dogs yet." Craig holds out his hand. "After you."

I start after the host. Allegro's is one of those places that

43

tries to be more classy than it is. They don't go so far as to use tablecloths, but the light fixtures are made of sparkly metal or just painted to shimmer. There's a statue of a Roman soldier in one corner, and the pictures over the booths are trying too hard. We pass one of a knight who may or may not have three arms, and I'm more than a little relieved that people are already seated beneath it.

The host deposits our menus at a booth, says something else in Italian, and leaves.

"I hope those weren't instructions for getting out in an emergency," Craig says, sliding onto one of the benches.

I sit across from him. "At least if it was, said instructions are short."

"Maybe." He opens his menu. "For all we know, that one word was a ten-page booklet."

"That would be unfortunate." My next remark about how we should consider leaving now just in case lodges in my throat. It doesn't want to be said because …. It can't be. I pinch my leg under the table. Nothing changes, which is weird. I don't want to make a joke about leaving because he might take it too seriously, and I don't want this to be over yet. I'm actually having fun.

Chapter 7: Craig

S o far, so good. This is the best date I've ever been on, even though it's only been about ten minutes. That should be weird, considering Molly looked like she wanted to be anywhere but here when she got out of the car that she didn't drive. That's also weird. Why did someone drop her off? Is she getting a ride back? Does she not have a car?

Wow, what's wrong with me? It's not the time to be thinking about all this stuff. I've been silent for a while. She's going to think I don't want to talk. At least I have a menu as an excuse for being anti-social.

"Good evening." A dark-haired waitress stops at our table and fills our water glasses. "Can I get you something to drink other than water?"

"No, thank you," Molly says without even a whisper of hesitation.

I scan the non-alcoholic beverages. Now isn't the time to appear irresponsible by drinking when she knows I need to drive. "I'll stick with water for now."

"All right." Waitress pulls a pad of paper and pen out of her pocket. "Are you ready to order, or do you need a few minutes?"

"I need a few minutes." It's my turn to not hesitate.

"So do I," Molly says.

Waitress puts the pen and pad away. "No problem. Take your time. I'll be back." She leaves.

I mumble a belated thank-you. The menu has me entranced. So many options.

Molly picks up her menu. "Do you know what you're going to get?"

Not a clue. "Probably something with pasta. Can't go to an Italian restaurant and not get pasta."

"You could." She flips to the pasta page. "But you're in luck. They do, in fact, serve pasta."

I snort, which is possibly the most embarrassing sound I've ever made. I cover it up by feverishly studying the pasta that they do, in fact, serve. And there's a lot of it. Two pages of premade dishes and a build-your-own, to be exact, and I have no idea what half of them are. "I'm not sure that's lucky."

Molly laughs, soft. It's a nice sound. "Let me guess, you don't know what the Italian words mean?"

Is she a mind reader? "Am I that obvious?"

"Only when you stare at your menu in abject horror." She points to the dishes and explains. Carbonara is oil, garlic, and egg with some vaguely Italian-sounding stuff. Piccata is a lemon sauce with stuff, and masala is a wine sauce with stuff.

"Thanks," I say when she finishes. "I don't know why they don't just put that on the menu."

"They assume people know." She shrugs. "Not a safe assumption to make in my opinion, but I work at A's. We believe in putting everything on the menu."

I remember the host who had to think about two plus three and shudder. A's has a good reason for spelling things out. "At least I can make an informed decision now."

"Ready to order?" Our waitress reappears with the impeccable timing that people suddenly develop when they go into the food-serving business.

Good thing I can make that informed decision. Despite this, I still stare at the dishes for a few minutes while Molly orders chicken masala with penne instead of linguini. I finally pick veal piccata with no substitutions. Waitress says that will be right out and takes our menus.

I let out a breath. "I'm glad that's over."

Molly smiles, which turns out to be as nice as her laugh, and folds her hands in her lap. "So, if we were five years older, I'd ask what you do for a living, but since we're not and you already know I'm a waitress, I'll ask what you do all day."

Ah yes, the tell-me-about-yourself part of the first date. I don't miss this part. "Well, during the school year, I do the school thing, and I start helping my uncle with construction in a couple of weeks."

"Glorious summer job?"

"Oh yeah." I shrug. "Glitz and glamour all the way."

"Sounds it." She takes a sip of water. "What are you in school for?"

"Psychology."

Molly's eyes go serious. "Looking to help people?"

Something like that. I'm looking to be a counselor for parents with wayward teenagers, but I can't mention that without bringing up Amber. And the evening's been going so well. I don't want to ruin it by thinking about, and thus worrying about, my sister. "Pretty much." I lean back in the booth. "So, what's your story? I've lived here my whole life, and I've never seen you before."

She stiffens and then starts to fiddle with her napkin. "My family moved here before I started high school, and I went to private school. Then I went to Mass State for college, graduated last month, and, well, moved back home." The speech sounds rehearsed, but it's impossible to tell if the show is for her or me. The fidgeting and staring at the table suggest the former.

"So that makes you, like, a whole year older than me."

"Something like that." Her voice is small and distant.

That's not a good sign. Did I say something wrong? And I'd just thought about how well this was going. It's time to start asking hopefully harmless questions. "What's your degree in?"

She perks up. "Graphic design, which is actually a lot more work than it sounds." Her tone is defensive, and I'm sure she's gotten crap about it "just being art" or something equally ridiculous.

I'm a firm believer that college is work no matter what, so in response, I point to the picture over our booth. It's of a girl fainting, badly, into her savior's arms. "So this must be your equivalent of nails on a chalkboard."

She winces. "That is just evil. I'm not a painter, but even my medieval concept art is better than that." She clamps her mouth closed, and her cheeks turn pink.

"You like medieval stuff?" Open mouth, insert foot. The blush is a sign of embarrassment, and there I go leaping on the topic that caused it.

She nods, slow. "A bit. It's fun stuff to work with."

Before I can respond, our waitress reappears with food. "Do you need anything else?" she says after setting down our plates.

Molly says we don't, which is good because I'm incapable of speech. I'm transfixed by my food. It's not the meat. That's fine. It's the pasta. Now I know why Molly substituted hers. I have linguine. Linguine as in the long, spaghetti-like stuff that requires fork-spinning talent. I don't have fork-spinning talent. The only things I can spin are lies when I'm playing a high-charisma character.

"All right," the waitress says. "I'll be back to check on you."

"Most likely when at least one of us has a mouthful of food," Molly says. "That's what I'd do." She forks a piece of pasta into her mouth and lets out a breath. "You aren't eating. Everything okay?"

I nod, still unable to form words, and pick up my fork. How does this work?

Molly exhales. "You have no idea how to twirl pasta, do you?"

Crap, she's found me out. I can't look dumb here. "Of course I do." I scoop up a forkful of noodles and flip my fork. They slide off and land in a pathetic clump on my plate. "Oops."

Molly fails to suppress her laughter, and my cheeks warm again. I'm destined to spend at least fifty percent of this date blushing, aren't I?

"Hey, I'm not Italian, and not everyone knows how to twirl pasta."

In response, she grabs my fork, scoops some linguine, and executes the kind of twirl an Olympic skater would be jealous of.

"My family's French," she says, handing me the fork.

I stare at the perfect little cocoon of noodles. "If you're so good at it, why did you order penne?"

She pauses with her fork halfway to her lips. "Because I know better."

Shut down.

The rest of dinner goes smoothly—well, as smoothly as me

with noodles can go. At least I don't end up wearing my food. By the end of the meal, my fork-spinning technique is no better, but Molly's gotten a few good laughs out of watching me try. There's no more sign of the blushing or quietness. She seems to be having fun, and that's all that matters.

"I'm never ordering noodle pasta again," I say after the waitress takes my plate.

"Never say never, Ms. Frizzle," Molly says in a passable imitation of one of the Magic School Bus kids. That shouldn't make the entire pasta-eating ordeal better, but somehow, it does.

The check comes, and I hand over my card. Molly's mouth falls open a little, and a tiny volcano erupts in my chest. She should not be surprised right now. What jerk took her out to dinner and didn't pay? Waitress brings back my card and the paperwork. I start to write in the tip, but Molly grabs my wrist.

"If you don't have small bills, I'll tip. We have to claim it if you write the tip in, and that's no fun. Trust me."

Another truth about waitresses confirmed—that unspoken rule to watch out for one another is apparently true. I put down the pen and hand her the check. "Go for it."

Her eyes go a little wide, but she doesn't say anything, just lays down cash. "Ready? It's—"

A familiar tune plays. It takes me a second, but I place it. Lords of Caldreth, that's the Lords of Caldreth theme, and it's coming from Molly's purse.

"You play Lords of Caldreth?"

She stares at her purse like it personally wronged her. Then she shakes her head. "Umm, yeah."

Chapter 8: Molly

Oh god. Oh god oh god oh god oh god, no. Shoot me now. I forgot to put my phone on silent, and now the entire restaurant knows I play Lords. Craig knows I play Lords. He's going to get all nerdy on me. The nice guy mask is going to disappear, and he's going to want to talk shop.

"I didn't think anyone played anymore." And there he goes. So much for this night. "I used to. I still have it on my phone, but time and such."

"Right." I pick up my purse, stand, and book it toward the front of the restaurant. I'm not going through two hours of him talking about gaming over the movie. Nikki will be miffed when I call her this early, but that's not my problem. It's time to cut my losses and run.

"We better get to the theater," Craig says behind me. "The movie starts in ten minutes." He moves beside me once we're through the door and pulls tickets out of his pocket.

My grand plan to ditch dies in infancy. He bought tickets. I'm getting dinner and the movie for free, and that meal wasn't cheap. Ward would have made up some excuse about being broke. Craig bought the tickets before he was even sure I'd be here.

51

I take mine as if it's poisonous. Pantheon, I can't walk out now. Walking out now would be the biggest jerk move ever. Never mind that using him to see the movie for free is also a jerk move. But I'm not just using him. So far, this has been fun. He's been a perfect gentleman. The only downer has been my phone going off, and he's already moved on. If he goes back to it, I can come up with an excuse for Lords, but I may not get another opportunity to see *Star Trek* with someone who loves it as much as I do. "Thanks."

"Welcome. Ready?"

I shove the ticket in my purse. The theater may only be a two-minute walk, literally, but I'm not risking losing the golden treasure. "Let's do this."

"Couldn't have said it better myself," Craig says. He waits for a family of five to pass and then steps into mall traffic. "So, Lords? I seriously didn't think anyone still played. You must love it."

That was fast. Though, it's not unexpected. Now I just need that excuse I was so proud of myself for thinking I could conjure. Crap, why didn't I major in communications or something that would have helped in these situations? Wait, that's it. "It's medieval." Thank the pantheon I slipped about my art preferences earlier. I can't believe I'm thankful for revealing my geek side. "I use it for inspiration. You don't think that's weird, do you?"

"Weird?" He spreads his hands. "I play Marshalls and Magics."

He has a point, but I can't say that and let him know how much attention I paid to his table last night. It's bad enough I looked at his ID long enough to remember his name. Saying I know he plays a wereclaw shifter shaman would be overkill and make me look like a stalker. "Oh, cool."

We reach the theater with seven minutes to spare—guess it's a three-minute walk. Craig takes my ticket when I get it out and presents them to the guy at the gate. The guy rips them and directs us to theater twelve. Like good economically and health-conscious movie-goers who just ate better food, we skip the concessions and head straight to the last door on the right. As late as we are, we still manage to get decent seats. This is helped by the fact that the theater isn't too crowded. There are some older folks down front—people who watched *Star Trek* when they were kids, probably. The mandatory battalion of teens has invaded and overtaken the back rows, and half of them are laughing twice as loud as is necessary. Craig points to the center portion of the theater. I respond by leading the way to a middle row.

"I hereby claim these chairs in the name of us," Craig says, flopping down.

I perch beside him. "How poetic."

The comfortable chatter from dinner returns, interrupted by the billion previews that blow our eardrums to bits. About ten minutes later, the please-don't-make-noise-or-litter announcement plays, and the lights dim. Then it's the Paramount Pictures logo, and we're boldly adventuring where no movie-goer has gone before.

We're with Kirk for a while, which is cause for silent fangirling. There is action and yelling, and then Nero blows up Kirk's father. After that, it's on to Vulcan. Spock makes his appearance, and the volume amps again. Sometime later, McCoy comes out. He starts talking, and the silent fangirling is no longer enough. I squeak like a communicator and clamp my mouth closed. I barely escaped the Lords inquiry. Don't blow it here. As covertly as I can, I glance at Craig. He shows no sign of hearing my moment, so I return my attention to the awesome before me.

The two hours fly by. Kirk, Spock, and the crew do their collective space-adventuring things. I swallow back more squeaks about McCoy and the special effects, and before I know it, the credits are rolling.

"Well," Craig says, standing and stretching. "That was quite awesome." His green eyes have the full-on Trekker glitter going.

Do mine look like that? I rub them just in case. "It was a good movie. Shall we?"

He nods, and I lead the way back down the stairs and toward the theater doors. Two teens are making out in the corner. I breeze past them—not letting people five years younger than me make me jealous—and open the door for Craig.

"Thanks," he says and joins me in the hall. "Anything else you wanna do?"

I yawn. What the heck? It's not even that late. It's just past ten. Nevertheless, I'm yawning. I guess yelling at Nikki took more effort than I thought.

Nikki ... who I now have to call to come get me. I do not want to stand around the theater and wait for her. I could get a ride with Craig, but if I don't have Nikki pick me up, she'll be all over me with awkward questions. Then again, she set me up on this, and while I had fun, it was still a setup. Let her wonder.

"I think I'm done for the night," I say after I finish yawning. "I have to work the lunch shift tomorrow."

"Ugh." Craig says. "Do you need to call for a ride? Or I can drive you home if you want."

Awesome, he just eliminated the creepy asking-for-a-ride process. Next time, I'm taking my car. "Could you? I don't feel like hanging around with all the tweens."

He laughs and pulls his keys out of his pocket. "Follow me."

We leave the building and wander into the sea of cars. The sky is black now, and I'm more than a little thankful for the streetlights, especially when it's clear Craig did not get a good parking spot.

"Where is your car?" I say when the mall is a good twenty feet behind us.

He points to a vehicle a few spots away. "Ta-da."

I blink. "You can afford that?"

He holds up his keys, and the car's lights flash. "This car is ten years old and was well-driven before I got it." He cuts in front of me and opens the front passenger door. "For you."

I stare for a second. I can't help it. In the two years we were dating, Ward didn't open a door for me once, and Craig's done it three times in one night. "Thanks." I slide into the car, which has freaking leather seats.

"Welcome." Craig closes my door and goes around. "Where do you live?" he says when he's backed out of the spot.

I give him my address. "Do you know where that is?"

"I've lived here my whole life. I hope so." He puts the car into drive and, well, drives.

I settle back into my seat and enjoy the smooth ride. Even at ten years old, this thing takes bumps well. That right there is worth not calling Nikki. I swear her car actually hits the ground when she turns.

"You know," Craig says when we're on the main road and cruising toward my neighborhood. "I was kind of hoping they'd have someone say beam me up. Scottie. Just because."

55

I snort. "Hah." My voice comes out a little squeaky. I clear my throat. "They'd probably have to get the rights from the billions of people who've misquoted the line."

"Probably."

I nod, not trusting myself to speak. Why do I sound like I took a dose of helium? That happens when I'm nervous, but there's nothing to be nervous about here. This date was actually fun. I'm on my way home. I can transform back into my mild-mannered, non-geeky true identity. For some reason, however, my hands take this as a cue to start trembling.

The rest of the ride is quiet, which is fine. I don't need to do my Minnie Mouse impression again. My body, however, thinks I need to be a rattle. The shakes expand outward from my hands until my arms and legs are shivering too. Seriously, what is this? I haven't been this nervous all night. I can't even remember the last time I was this nervous. A few turns later, we're at my house. Craig kills the engine and comes around to get my door, which is a good thing because my deep breathing exercises aren't working. It's a chore to contain my trembling on the walkway and even more on the stairs. I'm a leaf caught in a gale wind's storm. Ugh, and I'm writing bad poetry.

"I had fun," Craig says when we're standing on my front porch.

I nod and smile and dig out my keys, all while trying to look composed. This is not easy, and it takes a couple of tries to get the right key in the lock the right way. "Me too," I say when the door is unlocked. Post-hyperspeed-worthy shakes are no reason to be rude. "Thanks."

Craig nods, just staring at me.

My shakes increase to full-blown tremors. Is he going to kiss me? Oh god, what if he kisses me? Do I want him to kiss me?

The original Power Ranger's theme plays in his pocket.

That dispels my shakes, and a nervous laugh comes out. "Is that your text sound?"

"Yeah." He frowns at his pocket as if his phone can see it. His expression is a familiar one, though. It's the who-could-possibly-be-texting-me-now one. The next question is will he check, or will he ignore it because we're still technically on a date.

He pulls his phone out. Guess he's checking it. That's a point toward Ward territory. He reads for a second, and then his lips press into a flat line. He types a couple of words, his motions stiff and jerky, then puts the phone away.

"Trouble?" I say even though it's obvious.

"Family emergency." He takes my hand and plants a kiss on its back. "Till next we meet."

The shakes start all over again, now accompanied by prickles in my belly. This guy is either really old-fashioned, or he's just that level of geeky.

"Yeah." I let my hand fall back to my side. "Night."

Despite the family emergency, he waits till I'm inside before leaving. I manage to get the keys out of the lock and close the door without making a fool out of myself. Only after the rumble of his engine fades to nothing do the doubts begin. For all I know, that family emergency was his other girlfriend. That would be my luck. I finally meet a guy who's geeky and nice, and he would have another girlfriend.

"Hey, sweetie." Mom comes into the living room. Her hair is in its signature off-work ponytail.

Dad comes in behind her. "How was dinner?"

That's right. They don't know about the date because I didn't know about the date until I got to the date. And I really don't feel like telling them and getting the thousand questions. If there is a date number two and it goes well, I'll tell them. Until then, I'll just bend the truth a bit.

"It was fun."

"Good," Mom says, yawning. "We were on our way up to bed when we heard the car." She herds Dad toward the stairs. "Night."

"Night." I wait until their footsteps echo overhead before sagging into one of the chairs. If they'd seen the exchange on the porch and known it was post-date, they probably would have assumed it went badly. But it didn't go badly. At least, I don't think it went badly. It really was fun. Everything was going great until his phone went off, but I have no reason to believe it wasn't an emergency.

"Get a grip, Molls." Grip. The back of my hand pulses where his lips touched my skin, and a tingle runs through my body. I can't move for a second while the chill passes. No, the date went fine. If I'm having that kind of reaction to a kiss on my hand, things went better than fine. Thank the pantheon he didn't go for the real thing. I probably would have passed out. But what does it say that he didn't? What if he didn't want it? Or maybe he wants to wait until there's more time.

I press the back of my hand to my cheek and let out a long sigh. Either way, it feels a little too good.

Chapter 9: Craig

Goddam it, Amber!

It takes everything I have to keep control of the car. If she wasn't my sister, I'd kill her. I can't even blame Lyd for texting me and interrupting my date, not when she's apparently standing in front of my house with my sister and some random guy Amber brought home.

I take the turn onto my street practically on two wheels. A gaggle of teens stand on the corner. They jump back as I speed by, and one gives me the finger. Little punk, but I'm not stopping. Sure enough, there are lights on in front of my house. My headlights reflect off something—a car—a nice car that isn't Lyd's. My sister was in a car with this dude? My blood heats up, and I stop just short of ramming said car's bumper into oblivion.

Lyd is standing, arms folded, on my front lawn. She glances at me, and my fear and frustration are reflected in her expression.

I kill the engine and am out of the car and moving before I register locking the car.

"You bitch!" Amber rounds on Lyd, hand raised. "I can't believe you called him."

Oh hell no. I close the distance and grab Amber's wrist. "Actually, she texted me, and you can't believe something here? What are you doing with this loser?"

Amber glares at me. "Having fun. You familiar with the idea?" She rips free of my hold and leans back against loser. He wraps an arm around her waist.

I meet his gaze. He flinches a little but doesn't back down. Grow a pair, pal. "Are you familiar with the definition of statutory rape?" I ask as casually as if we met at the store, and I'm looking for Fig Newtons.

"According to her ID she's eighteen." He places a possessive hand on her breast. "So I don't know what—"

He doesn't finish the sentence. I have him away from my sister and pinned against his car with my knee at his groin.

"Craig." There's a warning note in Lyd's voice.

It brings me back from the edge, and I move my leg before I stop this guy from ever fathering children. "For your information, that's my sister, and she's fifteen."

Amber makes some kind of strangled noise.

"Wha …?" To the guy's credit, his face pales. He pushes me aside, not roughly, and holds out his hand to Lyd. "I'm not going to jail. Gimme my keys."

Lyd does—so that's how she kept him here—and he goes around to the driver's side.

Amber starts to follow, but I grab her before she gets two steps. She struggles, aiming her three-inch heel for my crotch. I dodge the move and drag her up the walkway, tossing my keys to Lyd. "Get the door?"

She catches them and cuts in front of me to do just that.

It's dark in the entryway. I hit the switch for the overhead light and shove Amber into the corner. Lyd closes and locks the door.

Which is apparently my sister's cue to get pissy. She lunges and shoves me back. "What is your problem?"

"My problem?" I push her away. In the light, her outfit is visible. She's wearing skinny jeans and a tube top that could be a hairband. Where does she get these clothes? I make a mental note to buy Lyd a present. I don't even want to know what would have happened if she hadn't driven by. "My problem? I go out one night, and I have to rush back here because my best friend sees you get out of a car with a guy who's way too old for you. Were you going to invite him in? Do you even know him?"

She huffs and stomps toward the stairs.

"Waiting for an answer," I say to her back.

"Good for you." She climbs the first three steps. "So here's one. None of your business! I'm not five anymore, and you aren't the boss of me." She pounds up the stairs. Just like last night, her bedroom door slams, and all goes silent. In the wake of the noise, my vision is every shade of red. It's not the anger that's killing me, though. My heart is pounding like crazy, and my stomach is in knots. Did Mom and Dad even know she went out tonight? Do they even care?

"Are you okay?" Lyd rests a hand on my arm.

I nod. I can't speak yet. What is going on with my life? My sister brought a guy my age home and then took a swing at my best friend. I breathe deep and face Lyd. "I'll survive. What about you? Did she hit you before I got here?"

"No." Lyd lowers her hand. "Her guy tried, but he's useless against a black belt."

I fist my hands and count to ten. It doesn't help, so I punch the wall. "Ow."

Lyd pats my head. "That was dumb. Seriously, you don't need to injure yourself over this."

She's right, but that doesn't cage the impulse much. I press my temples until my head hurts. Jesus, this is not okay. "I'm so sorry about this. You shouldn't be mixed up in my family's problems." I sink to the floor and bury my face in my hands. "I don't get it. Does she not care that I worry? And then she throws the fact that I'm not her parent into my face, as if she'd even listen to Mom and Dad. It kills that she doesn't think I'm worth listening to, though. Kills."

"I know." Lyd sits beside me and rubs circles on my back. "This shouldn't be your job."

I snort. "You're telling me." I blow out a long breath and straighten. "Thanks for randomly driving by my house."

"That's what friends are for, right?" There's strain in her voice. God, is this getting to her? This doesn't need to drag her down too. "I'm sorry you have to deal with this, and I'm sorry I interrupted you."

"It's all right." Though, really, it's not. I can't even have one night for me. Something twists in my gut. If I'm going to go on dates only to come home to some guy trying to do my sister against a car …. I shudder. "Mom and Dad need to step up. I mean, they have lives. I don't want to take that from them, but I'm not her father. And I can't be her father." My muscles tense. I need a change of subject. "You guys finished up awful early."

She's quiet for a second. "Technically, the game's still on. We took a break, and I decided to get some air."

She did? Why?

Before I can ask, though, the front door opens. Speak of the devils, my folks stroll in, Mom leaning on Dad for support.

Wonderful, she's drunk.

"Craig," Dad says, the word a little slurred. He's drunk too, and he probably drove. "We didn't think you'd be home so early."

"Well, I am," I say, digging my nails into my skin. So much for calming down. "Did you guys have fun, wherever you went?" I can't help it. The second half comes out derisive.

Mom straightens. "Yeah." Her slurring puts Dad's to shame. She takes a step on her own, wobbles, and leans against the wall. Her gaze roams the room before landing on me and then Lyd. "Oh, I didn't know your date was with Lydia."

I groan. Beside me, Lyd stiffens. If things weren't bad enough, now my parents are going to make this awkward.

"It wasn't." It's amazing how calm my voice is. "She—"

"It's about time, you know," Mom says, running her fingers through her hair. "You two have been so cute together for years."

"Right," I say. "Except—"

"Hope we aren't interrupting." Now Dad's gonna start too? "Don't let us keep you from taking things upstairs. You're old enough, Craig."

That does it. I stand and fold my arms. "Yeah, I know I am. Amber's not, though. I came home, and she had some random guy who was too old for her out front."

"Long as she didn't bring him in," Mom says. "No guys in the house."

I grit my teeth. The guy doesn't have to be in the house for something to happen, but I keep that thought to myself. My parents are too far gone to understand.

"But you two have fun," Mom says, sliding toward the floor.

Dad's at her side, holding her up. "Better get your mom

upstairs. My little wildcat had a little too much, if you know what I mean."

Mom laughs, a manic sound, and Dad guides her across the room and up the stairs. Somehow they get all the way up without falling to their deaths. Laughter and drunken encouragements of "just a bit farther" drift down to the foyer until their bedroom door clicks closed.

"I'm going to murder them," I say when it's quiet.

"No, you're not," Lyd says. "Because then you'll really be Amber's parent."

She has a point, and a bitter laugh escapes before I can stop it. "Yeah, and how messed-up would that be? I'm sorry about my mom, by the way."

Lyd blushes. We've been friends almost since birth, and of course, my mom picks tonight to get drunk and imply stuff about us. Not that Lyd isn't a great girl. I just don't like her that way.

"It's okay. It was a reasonable assumption for a sober person to make. So a drunk person …"

True, and to think the person who made that assumption is upstairs, clueless about how hurt I am. I can't stay here, not now. Amber's home. Mom and Dad are home, if drunk. I need a distraction. "Shall we join the game?"

"Sure," Lyd says, holding up her keys. "But I'm driving. You're prone to road rage right now."

Again, point.

We pile into her car. The drive to Dawn's is pretty quiet. I spend most of it analyzing the way we go. There are precious few reasons she'd get air by going from Dawn's house to mine, which makes me wonder if she drove by just to check on things. I make a mental note to upgrade that present I'm going to buy her.

Lyd parks when we get to Dawn's, and I buzz us in at the door. Dawn and I exchange a quick conversation, and we're admitted. We climb the stairs in silence and stay that way until Dawn lets us in.

"You have been gone longer than anticipated," she says, pointing to Lyd.

Lyd shrugs. "Life happened."

Dawn steps aside to let us pass. Immediately, Parker's voice reaches my ears. What is he going on about now?

"I see no problem with casting that spell, Dwarf." Is that Parker or Piff?

I enter the room. Parker has his arms folded, and Sonya is facedown on the table.

"Shifter?" Parker says, abandoning the mentally wounded Sonya. "Your presence is unexpected."

I shrug and sit. That's enough of an answer for now.

Parker doesn't give up. "Is this a sign that your evening did not go as planned?"

"Sure," I say. "Just not in the way you're thinking." I'm done thinking about my home issues.

Lydia sits next to me and pokes Sonya. "What did you do?" she says to Parker when there's no response.

"I did nothing," Parker says.

"Don't believe him." Sonya's voice comes muffled. She sits up, rubbing her eyes. "He's just being Piff."

"Enough." Dawn takes her GM seat. "Your companions have arrived. I will bring them up to speed." She looks from Lyd to me. "You are under attack from someone in a tower."

"Sounds about right," Lyd says.

"Okay." I grab Parker's D20, since I didn't even think to bring my dice, and roll. "Initiative ... nine." Nine? What is wrong with me lately?

Lyd rolls a fifteen, and Dawn shakes her head at me. "You will go last. Your turn, Elf."

Lyd does a decent amount of damage. Then someone hurls fire at us. Then it's my turn.

"I summon my spirit companion and umm, hmm?" Crap. "Can I summon my spirit companion in the air?"

Dawn blinks. Is she actually confused? "Excellent question."

"To which the mighty GM does not have an answer?" Parker says. Seriously, he's going to bring about his own slow death one of these days.

Sure enough, Dawn gives him the one-eyed stare. "That is enough, Puff." She clicks around on her laptop. "One moment."

Parker goes on about how his name is Piff, and I stare at the grid map. Our pieces are clustered around Dawn's rendition of a tower, which amounts to a long, narrow thing with a hole for a window where two pieces are placed to represent our attackers. It's all so medieval. Medieval, tower, Molly. If she likes Lords, she'd love M and M.

"The rules do not cover this inquiry," Dawn says, pushing her laptop aside. "Explain what you wish to do, and I will make a decision."

"Okay." Now, what exactly do I want to do? "Well, if I summon him up here at the window, can I attack one of these guys?"

Dawn is silent for a minute. "Possibly."

"You'd fall," Lyd says. "Does falling provoke an attack of opportunity?"

"Possibly," Dawn says.

I put my spirit companion token beside the guys in the tower.

It's a chance, much like tonight's date, and that went well. I'm in a chance-taking kind of mood, and I have a feeling that's going to carry over into next week. "I'm going to try it."

"Very well." Dawn makes a note. "Roll your attack."

I do and get a total of eighteen.

Dawn taps her chin. "Your companion makes a swipe at the tower but misses. It then plummets to the ground, where it soundlessly lands. Before disappearing, it glares at you."

Lyd, Sonya, and Parker burst out laughing.

I grin and remove the token from play. "It was a long shot." Hopefully, my chance-taking with Molly will go better than that.

Chapter 10: Molly

I check my makeup in the rearview mirror one more time. It's still there, so I let out one last breath and get out of the car. Tuesday mornings, much like Monday mornings, suck, and they double suck when occupied by job interviews scheduled the day before. I'm not complaining, though. I got an interview. It's the only one so far out of the thirty-five applications I submitted, and I'll take it.

I adjust my skirt. Beige has got to be the worst color on the face of the planet, and I look terrible in it. Unfortunately, it was the only job interview-appropriate item in my closet, which means, if I get this job, it's time for a shopping trip.

I make it across the parking lot only to almost trip over the curb. Okay, before shopping, I need to calm down. It's just a job interview. My hands start to shake. No, Molls. You're not doing this. You can't go in there shaking like a Polaroid picture.

And now that song's going to be stuck in my head. Though, maybe that's a good thing. Anything is better than hearing I'm doomed over and over again.

Despite the trembling, I make it to the building without a problem. Raydon's office is on the fourth floor. I get in the elevator, press the right button, and breathe. Sending them an application had been an afterthought. They'd popped up on my Google search, and I'd just applied. Go figure that they're the only ones to show interest.

The elevator stops. The door opens, and the shakes come back full force. A deep breath does nothing. Swallowing about four million times does nothing, so I trudge down the hall toward suite 403. It's a normal wooden door with a window that looks in on a normal office. I grip the knob, which is clammy ... or maybe that's me, and let myself inside. If I stand in the hall I'll never go to the interview, and I need to go to this interview.

"Good morning," a woman says from behind the secretary's desk. "Can I help you?"

I take careful steps until I'm standing in front of the desk. Somewhere in the back of my addled brain I realize the walls match my outfit. Will they see that as me getting on board with the company?

Focus. "Hi. My name is Molly Morreau, and I have a ten-o'clock appointment with Mr. Cage."

Secretary clicks around on her computer. "All right, have a seat, and he'll be right with you."

I sit in one of the very uncomfortable chairs and stare at the beige walls. These people need a designer. That thought replaces Polaroid picture—thank the pantheon—and soon after, a door opens.

"Molly?" a thirty-something man in a freaking beige suit says. He's going to think I spied on him and color coordinated.

"Yes." I stand and hold out my hand.

He takes and shakes, surprisingly firmly. "I'm John Cage." Seriously? "Come on back."

I follow him down a beige hallway to his beige office and sit in the beige chair in front of his brown desk. Finally, some color.

"So." He sits behind said desk. "You just graduated from Mass State with a degree in graphic design?"

Is that my cue to talk? That's my cue to talk. I clear my throat and force words out. "Yes. In May." Which is on my resume. Awesome job.

John nods as if I've given him new information. "So why graphic design?"

My mouth goes dry. "Well." Great start. "I, umm, I like digital art because I have no regular art talent to speak of."

He laughs. He actually laughs. I'm either hilarious when I'm half brain-dead, or he feels that bad for me. "Why our company?"

I brace myself for more brain-deadness, but apparently my intelligent self is waking up. "I agree with your philosophy on excellence, and I want to be part of a workforce that takes a go-getter approach to graphics." Holy crap. Did I say that? Go me. I open my mouth again, and more good-sounding stuff comes out.

When I finish, John leans back in his chair. He might even look impressed. He fires a few more questions, and I respond, coherently. Maybe I have a shot at this job, after all.

"When could you start?"

"Immediately." Except for that waitressing job I have to quit first. Brain, what happened? You were doing so well. "Well, not quite immediately. I'm working as a waitress to pay the bills now, but I'm prepared to switch."

John nods, stiff.

Crap. Only my need to maintain an air of professionalism

keeps me from burying my face in my hands. I blew it. That was the worst answer in the history of answers.

"Well, I don't have any more questions," John says. "Do you have any for me?"

I did, but they're gone now. Fail is back on loop in my brain. The voices are announcing Kid Chameleon's death. "Not that I can think of."

John stands. I stand. He says something about being in touch. I shake his hand and say something that sounds like thank you. He walks me out. I keep my composure until I'm downstairs. Then I walk like Sonic on speed to the car, where I sit in the driver's seat and let my stupidity wash over me. What was that? That was the worst interview ever. The only saving grace is that I don't have time to analyze it. I have to get to A's.

The five-minute drive is over in a flash. I park Dessy and jog to the back door. The restaurant isn't technically open yet, which is convenient. I change into my uniform in the bathroom and wander back to the kitchen to come face to face with Nikki.

"Hi there," she says, way too cheery. "So how've you been? How's life?" Irritated best-friend-who's-been-ignored pours off every word.

I brush past her to punch in my shift. The squirmy feeling in my stomach from Friday hits me all over. A combination of not talking about it and the job interview had kept it away, and now that I've lost both distractions, it's back to torment me. At least I can control one of those. "I don't think I got the job."

Nikki waves a hand. "Not that part of life. Someone had a date Friday night and didn't give me details all weekend."

I suppress a snort. As if I have a hope of steering Nikki off a topic she wants to be on. "The date was okay."

"Just okay?"

"Ladies, I need one of you at the hostess desk," our shift leader says, blessedly interrupting the conversation.

I plant my finger on my nose. "Not it."

Nikki scowls. "Fine. But we will finish this conversation later."

Lucky me.

A's opens, and shortly after, the lunch rush swarms. I take orders for three tables and settle into the pattern of waitressing. I won't miss this. That thought should startle me, but it doesn't. I'd give a lot to get out of here and have a better paying job doing what I love. I'll just have to wait for the next opportunity.

The first order comes up, and I take the salad and chicken club for table seven. Nikki gives me a warning glare when I pass her. The host finally showed up ten minutes late, relieving Nikki of replacement duty and putting her back into interrogation mode. I offer her an innocent smile and throw myself into work, only popping into the kitchen when absolutely necessary. If I can keep this up until my shift ends, I'm golden. The last thing I need is Nikki calling bull on Craig's text when I want to believe that it really was a family emergency, and not another girl, for a little longer.

"I know you're ignoring me," Nikki says the next time we cross paths. Perceptive, she is. "I will make you talk."

"Eventually," I say too soft for her to hear and scurry out into the dining room with the burgers for the father and daughter at table twelve. They thank me, and I take my time checking on all my other customers. If there's one thing waitressing has taught me, it's stalling, and I'm a Jedi master at it.

I turn from table nine—three teen girls—and a blast of hot air hits me. Typical of summer in New England, the temperature today is about twenty degrees hotter than yesterday. The sun reflects off the swinging front door, blurring everything by the host stand. The door closes, and the fog clears. I stop shielding my eyes.

Craig and two of his friends—spiky hair and the brunette—are here.

I make some kind of squeaking noise and book it back to the kitchen.

"Knew you couldn't stay out there forever." Nikki's waiting beside the door.

I rush past her and busy myself reading the order list. What is he doing here? Is he here to see me? I haven't talked to him since Friday night.

Nikki pokes my arm. "Well, details. And why are you doing the read-orders-and-hide thing?"

Because Craig's out there with friends, and I don't know if he knows I'm here. He can't know I'm here. He wouldn't bring friends if he knew I was here and came to see me. Or did his friends drag him, and he doesn't even want to see me? Or does he even remember or care that I work here? Maybe he decided to date the brunette, and they brought spiky-hair dude as a supplemental offering?

"Molls?" Nikki snaps her fingers in my face. Her nails are aqua today.

I swallow. "Craig's out there." And then I bite my tongue. What is it with me and blurting things about him around her?

"And you're in here why?" Nikki grips my shoulders and all but drags me toward the door.

I dig my heels in, but it's no use. I need to start going to the gym more often. "Nikki, don't. I—"

"You what? Don't tell me you're embarrassed."

"No, I—" Crap, I'm gonna have to tell her. "I'm not sure where I'm at with him."

Nikki halts and faces me. "What do you mean, you're not sure? Either the date went well or it didn't. I'm not sure because someone's been avoiding me."

I pretend not to hear the jibe. "Well, yeah." This is going to suck. "But it ended kind of … abruptly."

"And you didn't tell me the nanosecond you got home?" She plants me in one of the chairs beside the door. "Explain."

Looks like there's no way out of it now. I take a deep breath and spill.

Nikki's eyebrows start rising and don't stop till I finish. "Sounds like an excuse, but his reaction seems real the way you're describing it. I say give him another chance."

My heart does a victory lap, deftly ignoring my orders to knock it off. *Sounds genuine,* not *is genuine.* That's not the same thing. The part of me that blushed over a kiss to my hand, though, doesn't give a flying monkey's butt.

"You sure?" I say.

"Yeah," Nikki says, pulling me out of the chair and shoving me toward the door. "And I know you too well, Molly Moreau, to fall for the nervous routine. You wanna give that boy another shot." She grabs the water pitcher off the counter beside the door and thrusts it into my hand. "Now, get out there and take his order."

I stumble out the door, biting back a *yes, ma'am.* That would only empower her, and that's the last thing I need. The distance from the kitchen to Craig's table stretches forever. Who cast the warp distance spell? And the muffle surroundings spell? Not that either of those exists in real life, but they sure feel real now. Tingles fly up and down my body, and I trip over the floor. What the hell's wrong with me? I went on one date that didn't even end with a kiss. Or maybe that's the problem. How do I interact with him now? Do I pretend I haven't seen him since Thursday and act like I don't recognize him? Do I greet him by name and smile at his friends?

Do I run back to the kitchen and demand Nikki take his table?

That holds a lot of appeal, and I'm about to do it when Craig looks up, right at me.

A's freezes. For a minute, it's as if every customer's eyes are on me, watching the awkward waitress and the cute guy she went on a date with. I hold my breath.

Craig grins, just a *hey* grin. It's not awkward. It's not uncertain.

Maybe this won't be awful, after all.

I start forward again. While I was frozen, the rest of the world wasn't, Craig's tablemates no exception.

"So the orc said 'little gnome creature good for eating,'" spiky-hair dude is saying. "So I raised my spell book and shouted, 'I command thee piff from existence.'" He bursts out laughing, snort and all. "Get it, piff instead of poof because my name is Piff?"

Craig meets my eyes again, and there's a desperate plea for help this time.

It's my turn to grin. I finish my journey to his table and commence filling water glasses. "How are you guys doing today?"

Spiky-hair dude makes a high-pitched noise and practically leaps out of his chair. Craig bites his lip, probably to hold back a laugh, and the girl nods.

"We're good," Craig says. He doesn't leer or look at me in any weird way.

The last of the tension in my stomach fades. "Can I get you drinks?"

The girl orders cranberry juice, and the boys get sodas. No one tries to order a free misspelled drink this time, and I make my retreat.

"See," Nikki says when I'm back in the kitchen. "That wasn't so hard."

I glare. She winks and rushes through the door. It wasn't hard, no. It was surprisingly easy, which should possibly worry me. I get the cranberry juice and go to the edge of the bar to get the sodas.

"Thanks for the save," Craig says beside me.

I almost drop the glass. Only my years of waitressing experience and an eighteen dexterity keep me from taking a shower in the stuff. I place the drinks down and face him. "You scared the life out of me."

"Sorry." He gives an abashed grin. "I wanted to catch you away from too many people. I have a question."

Question? This is either very good or very bad. I lean against the bar. "Okay, shoot."

He glances around and leans closer. "Do you have any interest in playing Marshalls and Magics?"

All the air goes away. I try to breathe, but nothing happens. Marshalls and Magics—why is he asking me about Marshalls and Magics? Did I give off more of a geek vibe than I meant to? Did I tape one of my old char sheets to the back of my work uniform in my sleep and then wear that shirt today without noticing?

"Marshalls and Magics?" Nikki appears as if summoned by

an inconvenient-arrival-of-unwanted-person spell and starts filling a drink. "Didn't you used to play that, Molls?"

Oh my god. I'm going to kill her. I'm going to send an assassin or fry her with a fireball or invoke divine justice, depending on what character I'm playing. She did not just announce that in front of Craig. Though I shouldn't be surprised after the setup she pulled Friday.

"You did?" Craig's eyes light up with some really intense form of hope.

I shove the second glass under the drink fountain. Damage control time. "I played a little in college. It was okay."

"You said you liked it," Nikki says. Okay, she can leave any time now. "I even played a few times. It's fun. Go for it." She finishes filling a glass, winks, and retreats, leaving me face-to-face with the gamer geek.

"So," Craig says. "Do you want to give it another shot?"

I bite my lip. The problem is that I do want to play. I enjoyed it. Nikki's right, but that was before Ward made it a torture session. What if that happens again? What if Craig's okay the first few times but then starts to be an jerk? I can't get trapped again.

I put down the glass and watch him. He really looks hopeful, and a poisoned dart hits home in my chest, delivering the moment's undeniable truth. I can't say no with him like that. My conscience won't let me.

"Sure." That one word grates across my tongue like reluctant sandpaper, but I can't bring myself to take it back. "When do you guys play?"

The hopeful light in his eyes blooms into a white dwarf star. "We don't have an exact schedule, but our next session is on Thursday."

Of course it's on a night I'm not working. I'm really not getting out of this. That is, if I actually want to get out of it. "Sounds good. I have Thursday night off." That came out more excited than I wanted.

"Awesome." He matches my enthusiasm. "We can make you a character and such sometime before then. I'll text you." He points to the drinks. "Now, though, I'll let you get back to your job."

My cheeks warm. I forgot I was even at work. Smooth move, considering I'm going to need to keep this job for a while. "Right. I'll have your drinks over in a minute."

"I'll keep an eye out for them." He winks and saunters away.

I watch him go, and my legs start to shake. What the hell's wrong with me? Okay, he's cute and nice, he's a geek, and no thanks to my soon-to-be-dead best friend, I'm going to see him in gamer action in two days. This is not cause for girliness.

"That looks like it was a productive conversation." Seriously, does Nikki stand around the kitchen and wait for me to report?

I shift the cups so the tops point at her. "I hate you."

She grins. "No, you don't. You want to spend time with that boy. Now bring him his drink." She's gone before I can respond.

I straighten the drinks. I do not want to spend time with him. Okay, I do, but not like this, not yet, not until I'm sure he's not Ward.

Then again, not taking chances only holds one back, and I got out of one Ward situation. If I absolutely have to, I can get out of a second. But whether I can get out of it with my heart intact is another question.

Chapter 11: Craig

I park at Dawn's apartment complex and kill the engine. The last two days passed in a flurry of texting Molly to make plans and nervous anticipation. We decided to meet an hour before game time to make her a character, which is why she's sitting beside me while I breathe and hope this goes well. "Ready?"

"Yeah." Her voice isn't overly excited, but it's not full of dread either. She gets out of the car.

I follow suit and lead the way across the lot. Part of me still can't believe I talked Dawn into adding a fifth person to the group. Four—one for each group role—is the sweet spot for a campaign, but I had to get Molly in on this. This is the game of games for people who play Lords and like medieval stuff. It's a match made in her afterlife location of choice.

"This place is nice," Molly says when we enter the pre-foyer.

I punch in the code to call Dawn's apartment. "That it is." The box rings.

"Hello," Dawn says in the voice she uses when not talking to the group. It's normal enough to not make people run for their lives.

"It's me," I say.

There's a pause, and the door clicks open. "Enter." There's the real Dawn. The box goes dead.

I open the door and gesture for Molly to go ahead.

She does, a little slowly. "That was ominous."

I follow her into the building. "That's Dawn. Stairs or elevator? We're going to the second floor."

Molly goes to the stairwell door, and I fall just the tiniest bit in love with her. I hate elevators for short rides. I join her, catching my reflection in the mirror over a pair of plaid chairs and wooden table. I don't know how many times I've visited Dawn since she moved here six months ago, but Molly's right. The place really is nice, especially for someone just out of college. The walls are white, granted, but white walls are easy to deal with when the front door actually locks and has a security system. The green carpet is reasonably plush, and the furniture, though ugly, has provided a decent place to sit on occasion.

We climb the steps in the equally clean stairwell, and I open the door when we reach the second floor. Molly thanks me, and we start down the hall, which is also clean. I stop in front of apartment 209 and knock.

Dawn opens the door almost immediately. She's in her standard combat boots and dark clothes. "Enter."

I hide a flinch. That's even more ominous in person. I'm a big tough shaman, though. I go inside and pause to wait for Molly's initial reaction. Dawn's place can take a little getting used to for non-motorcycle and tattoo people. The posters reflect the first, and the drawing pads, spread like dog toys, hold designs for the second.

Molly's eyes go a little wide. "Whoa." Her voice is almost a whisper. "This place is intense."

"Many thanks," Dawn says. She crooks a finger and clomps toward the spare room.

Molly halts beside a poster of some black-leather-and-guns chick and swallows, hard. "I think I'm afraid."

"You should be," Dawn says from the other room.

Molly's face loses some color.

I take her arm and guide her forward. "Don't fear. Dawn's all bark."

"On the contrary, Shifter." She pokes her head around the doorframe. "You have simply not seen the teeth yet. Enter, sit."

All right, maybe Dawn's a little terrifying.

Regardless, Molly and I enter and sit. Dawn clicks around on the internet for a minute before logging into the online builder and starting a new character. "Are you familiar with the available class and race options?"

"I want a changeling rogue with a specialty in stealth and theft."

Dawn raises an eyebrow, and I clench my jaw to keep it from dropping open. Holy fighter-class, Batman. Played a little in college? That is not how someone who played a little in college talks. I've known people who play a little. They stammer like crazy when asked about race and class.

"Done," Dawn says. "Now, ability scores."

The next hour flies. Molly spends a good portion of that time finagling over her dexterity score, but that's understandable. She's a rogue, after all. Scores set, they move on to skills and bonuses and attacks. Molly makes quick, informed decisions about each, and with every choice, something about her changes. Her eyes shine, and she sits up straighter, fidgeting replaced by more flowing movements. It's all I can do to pay attention to the conversation and not scoot closer to her. She flips her hair in my direction once, and cherry fills my nose.

God, I'm hooked.

"Very well," Dawn says sometime later, scaring the wits back into me. She clicks the builder's print button, and her ancient printer sputters to life. Molly's character sheet comes chugging out. "Changeling rogue with stealth and theft specialties. Thirteen strength, eighteen dexterity, twelve constitution, eleven intelligence, ten wisdom, sixteen charisma." She hands the papers to Molly. "You should be able to climb a wall and convince a hoard of goblins not to kill your friends at the same time without too much difficulty. Not, that you will have to do this."

That wakes me fully from my Molly-induced trance. Thank whoever's listening that Dawn isn't in charge of my real life.

Molly reads for a minute. "Looks good. When do we start?"

With the timing only possible in bad sitcoms, the call box for the building door buzzes.

"Now." Dawn stands and leaves the room.

"Convenient," Molly says, voice soft. She lays her character sheet on the table and rubs circles on her temples. The sparkle in her eyes is gone, replaced by a glassy stare.

What the heck? "You ok?"

She flinches. "Yeah, fine." The answer is a little too fast. "Just … nervous. I haven't played in a while, and I'm afraid I'll mess up or forget the rules or just roll bad numbers or—"

"You won't." I put my hand over hers where it rests on the table. "Everything's gonna be great."

Something crashes in the hallway, and we both jump, hands flying apart.

"So I see," Molly says.

There's a string of noises that might be words, and then

Parker steps into the room. He's carrying a box that's half as tall as him and, for some reason I cannot fathom, holding it so it blocks his face.

"Is this the den?" he says.

"Yes." I stand and take the box.

"Ah, that's much better," Parker says. "And good to see you, Shifter friend. I see you have brought your fair maiden."

Behind me, Molly giggles.

I hold onto the box. If my hands are full I can't strangle the gnome. "I did, and you brought what?" I shake the box. A soft rattling comes from inside.

"Behold." Parker opens it to reveal a family-sized pack of gummy bears and similar snacks.

"Is it not perfection?" Parker grabs a bag and holds it up. "There is, as the label suggests, enough for the whole family."

"Yeah, if you're the Brady Bunch on steroids." Lyd saunters into the room, moving Parker out of the doorway. "Hey, Craig." Her gaze fixes on Molly, and her eyes widen.

I toss the box aside—no sense in taking care with it now—and face the girls. "Lyd, this is Molly. Molly, this is Lydia—our resident elf."

Molly stands and offers her hand. "Nice to meet you."

Lyd eyes Molly's hand as if it's the hand from the old Kid Chameleon video game. Probably should have told her about Molly coming ahead of time. Lyd's not great with surprises. Finally, she takes and shakes. "Likewise." She releases and sweeps around the table to sit across from me.

"Where are the rest?" I say.

"Right here." Dawn enters with Sonya in tow and closes the door. She really does have that ominous timing thing down. "Retrieve any nourishment you may desire now. We begin momentarily."

We all take our seats, except for Parker. He grabs about fifteen bags of gummy bears and then sits across from Molly.

Sonya gives him the evil eye. "If you talk with your mouth full this time, I'll be having Piff stew for dinner."

"Moving on." Thankfully, Dawn also has the interrupting thing down. "As you have no doubt noticed, we have a new member. This is Waven Ringcaster, rogue changeling, and she will be joining your party shortly, after she completes a small encounter of her own." Dawn turns the full force of her black-eyelinered gray eyes on Molly. "Are you ready?"

Molly sits straight and stares right back. "Do your worst."

The rest of us exchange bewildered stares. Molly just signed her death warrant, and it tugs, hard, at my heart.

"Very well. Though you may live to regret those words." Dawn slaps a token on the map. "You begin in the plains. You've heard tell of a city near here, but you are not sure either of its name or direction from your current position. You passed a band of travelers a few miles back but did not ask them. You are wary. The sun hangs low in the western sky. There is a cluster of trees, perfect for camp, that you think you can reach by nightfall." Dawn sits back in her chair.

Molly hums to herself and eyes the map. So she's the concentrating type. "I'll make for the trees." She moves her token forward.

"Stop." Dawn's command freezes the room. "You hear a shout to the east. Roll perception."

Molly picks up her D20 and lets it fall. No elaborate shaking or dancing. "Fifteen, twenty-four with bonuses."

Seriously? It's her first roll, and she gets a natural fifteen? I've barely managed to roll over 10 since we started the campaign.

"You are able to discern that the voice is male and in trouble," Dawn says. "It is the shout of surprise most often given when one is attacked. These may be the only other living beings you encounter. It is not likely they know who you are, and they can most likely direct you to the city."

Molly's silent for a moment, staring at the board. "I guess I'll go toward the sound."

Dawn grins. "Wise decision."

We're screwed. That grin never means anything good.

"You make haste toward the noise. After about five minutes, you crest a hill to see two groups at battle. Four—indistinguishable from this distance—are surrounded by what appears to be goblins or kobolds."

"Hate kobolds," Molly says under her breath.

"Me too," I say. Who knew we had kobold hatred in common.

"The creatures make another attack, and a small humanoid rises above their heads. It shouts something about puffing and then rains down minor destruction."

Parker blinks. "Is that me? My name is—"

Sonya clamps a hand over his mouth. "Shut up and eat some gummy bears."

Molly makes a snorting noise and bites her lip. At least she finds Parker amusing. "I change appearance and move toward the battle. The little puffing creature is cute, and I feel bad."

Parker turns purple and wrenches free of Sonya's grip. "Puff is not cute! I mean, Piff is not cute!"

That does it. The entire room collapses into fits. I fold over the armrest, gasping. I can't stop, and I see stars. Normal breathing is out of the question. Hell, I can't even move. It's a good thing Dawn bought real chairs and not the benches she'd wanted. I'd be on the floor with a concussion. I lean forward in an attempt to get back some control and lock gazes with Molly. Her eyes are sparkling, and her smile is huge. It makes me laugh even harder, if such a thing is possible. She's happy … and beautiful.

"All right, children," Dawn says when she's mostly under control. "Let us continue. Changeling, what course of action do you take next?"

Molly coughs and takes a deep breath. Even so, her voice still shakes a little. "I'll use my sneak attack."

"Very well." Dawn does something on the computer. "Roll stealth."

Molly tosses her D20. "Seventeen plus nine … twenty-six." She must have magic dice.

"More than enough," Dawn says. "Move into position and roll your attack."

With the confidence only displayed by experienced players, Molly navigates the map, choosing the most tactical spot possible. She has partial concealment and a clear shot. Another toss of the die results in a sixteen attack roll, which is just enough to hit. She takes out one of the creatures, and Dawn removes the token from play.

"Minions," Sonya says, her voice full of triumphant glee. "Even better."

"You still have partial concealment, but the creatures are alerted to your presence," Dawn says. "Elf, it is your turn."

"Minor action perception check," Lyd says without hesitation. She snatches her D20 and lets it fall. "Nineteen plus nine is twenty-eight." Her triumph puts Sonya's to shame.

"You see someone in the shrubs," Dawn says. "But you can't tell much about them."

Lyd snorts. "Sounds about right. Attack." She rolls a two and punches the table. "Son of a bugbear."

"I know the feeling," I say.

She glares at me as if the bad roll is my fault and then moves her character token one square. "Move action shift. End of my turn."

Dawn points to Parker. "Gnome."

Parker takes his turn, then Sonya, then me and so on. I roll a three—so much for my D20 getting over its issues—and pass the torch to Molly. The battle takes too long to win, and by the time it's over, I'm out of my more powerful healing spells, and Sonya has to take three of her hit-point boosts.

"Well, that sucked," Lyd says. It's impossible to tell if she's speaking as herself or Kobri.

"'Agreed,'" Sonya says, definitely in character as Cathra. "'But I believe we owe part of our victory to an unseen friend.' I hale the newcomer and approach the shrubs. "'Come out, there.'"

"I hesitate but come out," Molly says. "But I make sure I'm in a shape I've never used before."

Sonya bows her head. "I bow to our savior. 'Many thanks for your aid, stranger. What is your name?'"

"'Waven,'" Molly says. Hearing it from her lips, it's perfect for her. "'And you're welcome.'"

"'We are in your debt,'" Sonya says. "'Is there anything we may do to even the score?'"

"'Dwarf.'" Lyd practically hisses. She's really getting into character.

"'There is,'" Molly says before Legolas and Gimli can go at it. "'I seek a group to travel with temporarily. I ask that you ask no questions. In return, I will aid you in any way I can and take my leave at a time that is convenient for you as well as me.'"

"'One moment,'" Sonya says. She holds up her index finger, our signal for group powwow—and turns to bring Parker into the conversation. "'What do you think? This seems an opportune opportunity.'"

"'Superb use of the language,'" I say. "'As for an answer, I see no reason not to.'"

Lyd folds her arms. "'Except for the obvious ones. Such as, can we trust her?'"

"'She just saved our lives,'" I say.

"'We barely know her,'" Lyd says, and for some reason, she sounds more like herself than her character.

I spread my hands. "'We barely know each other.'"

"'Here, here,'" Sonya says.

Lyd picks at the edge of the map but says nothing.

"'That's three of us.'" Sonya faces Parker. '"What say you, Gnome?'"

Parker holds up a gummy bear. "'So long as she agrees to call me by my true name, I have no objections.'" Then he pops the bear in his mouth.

Sonya rolls her eyes but maintains her composure. "'It is decided, then. You may travel with us, Waven.'"

"'Thank you, good company,'" Molly says. Her voice is strong and confident and perfectly in character. She brings comfortable-in-a-role to a whole new level. "'I am in your debt.'"

Chapter 12: Molly

Dare I say it, I'm actually having fun. This is nothing like the crushed-in-a-trash-compactor experience that playing with Ward and company was. This is fun and free and easy. Craig's group works well together. They have some awesome characters, and they've brought me right into the game and made me feel welcome. Well, except for Lydia, but she keeps rubbing her eyes and forcing her head up. I think her lack of enthusiasm is because she's tired.

The next three hours fly. Dawn sends us around to kill everything from goblins to drakes. It's a massive xp fest, and at exactly 12:01, she announces that we've reached level two. Cheers go up around the table, everything from Sonya's *we rock* to Parker's *long live gummy bears*. Craig holds his hand up in Lydia's direction. She hesitates but finally gives him a half-hearted high five.

"Well done, adventurers," Dawn says. "Do you wish to continue or end for the night?"

"End," Sonya says around a yawn. "Some of us have summer jobs in the morning."

Lydia stands. "Second."

"Very well." Dawn closes her books and laptop. "We will

discuss our next meeting later. Now, all of you leave my sanctum."

Craig pauses mid rolling up the map. "Yes, ma'am."

We collect everyone and stagger soberly downstairs and out to the parking lot. There's a chorus of *farewell gnome/elf/dwarf/shifter/changeling,* and Parker and Sonya go left, leaving Craig, Lydia, and I to go right.

"Where are you parked?" Craig says to Lydia.

Lydia shrugs and waves toward the rear of the lot where there are no streetlamps. "It's the only spot I could find."

Craig purses his lips. We pass his car, but he keeps walking. He's a gentleman.

"You don't have to walk me to my car," Lydia says. "I'm not fifteen."

Craig grunts as if someone punched his stomach, and his shoulders slump. "I know." His voice is so quiet. "But I am anyway."

Lydia doesn't respond. When we reach her car, she beeps it unlocked and faces him. "How are things at home?" There's concern in her voice but something else too.

This time, Craig's entire body sags. "The same." He opens her door and waits.

Lydia stares at him for a long time. Finally she pats his shoulder. "Call me if you need anything." She gets in and lets him close the door. A minute later, she starts the engine and drives away.

Craig watches the car's retreat. When it's out of sight, he shakes his head and starts back across the lot. "Shall we?"

I fall into step beside him. The comfortable silence from the other night is gone, replaced by something as thick as peanut butter-laced fog. What did Lydia mean about things at home?

And why does Craig look like he wants to sink into the concrete and never rise again?

At his car, he holds the passenger door for me before getting in and starting the journey to my house. Once the tick-tick of the blinker is gone, the silence starts and stretches.

"What did she mean?" I say when I can't take it anymore. Then I bite the inside of my mouth. This is clearly not the time to ask. Besides that, as he pointed out earlier, we barely know each other.

He keeps his eyes on the road with an almost tangible vengeance. "Just family issues. Lyd's been helping with them for a while." The words are finite.

"Oh." So the family emergency was probably real, then. That fills me with more relief than I expected. I search for something more to say, but nothing comes, and if I'm honest, that might be a good thing. So far, this friendship is based on Nikki setting me up, twice. Whatever's between us has the consistency of cracked glass. One tiny movement will shatter it, and as crazy as it sounds, I'm not interested in breaking anything here, geekiness considered. "Gotcha."

He nods, and the silence returns, still thick and uncomfortable. I settle back in my seat and watch the streetlamps pass. As is often the case, the ride home seems to take less time than the ride to the original destination—never mind that it's the same distance at roughly the same speed—and ten minutes later, Craig parks in front of my house. Mom's car is in the driveway, but the house is dark. She and Dad are probably asleep, which is fine. I open my door the second Craig kills the engine. Now isn't the time to play damsel. He walks me up the front steps, and we just stand on the porch.

"Well, I had fun." The words don't leave a sour taste in my

mouth or make the little voice in my head scream something about not lying. I forgot how much fun being geeky can be. I dig my keys out of my purse and insert the right one in the lock. This is a major improvement over the fumbling shakes from the other night. "Thanks for inviting me."

"You're welcome." His voice is soft and distant. He doesn't look at me, just stares at nothing.

My stomach clenches. Is he distant because I didn't ask about his family issues? Was I supposed to ask about them? He gave off the don't-want-to-talk-about-it vibe, but Ward used to do that all the time and then get pissed when I didn't ask. And there I go, overanalyzing. I'm going inside and ending this night before I say or do something stupid. "I guess I'll see you at the next session. Now that I know where Dawn lives, I can drive myself. That is if—"

Craig closes the distance and stops my rambling with a kiss.

Butterflies explode in my stomach. It's like the freaking big bang in there. His arms go around my waist, and he pulls me closer. Oh, that feels good, too good. A kiss hasn't felt this good in forever. Before I can stop myself, I rest my hands on his shoulders and lean in. He doesn't take that as any kind of sign. He doesn't try to get his tongue in my mouth. He doesn't try and feel up under my shirt. His hands stay absolutely still. We stay absolutely still, except for the gentle pressure and slight movements of our lips. The big bang is over, and a new sun has formed with me at its center. There's heat and light and the cozy warmth of melted chocolate, which doesn't belong on a star. It doesn't matter, though. This is our universe, my sun, and I'm a pile of nuclear goo in Craig's arms.

Too soon, it's over. Craig is pulling away, and I'm clinging to him. I lower my hands before I make a fool out of myself.

"Good night," he says. His voice is low and a bit ragged, and his green eyes are pools of forest.

Shooting stars fly through my blood. When was the last time a guy sounded that breathless around me? "Night." I fumble behind me. Where the hell is the doorknob? It needs to be in my hand, like now. What feels like forever later, I find it and turn it. Thank the pantheon I unlocked it before the kiss. I bite off a sigh and let myself inside, pulling the keys out and closing the door in record time.

The living room is dark, which I noted already. It feels like new information, though. Anything I knew or learned between leaving Dawn's and this moment is new. I blink. It doesn't help. I should turn a light on, but my legs aren't ready to move yet.

Craig's footsteps echo on the wood of the slats, and I lean back against the door. My eyes flutter closed, and I can feel him against me again. His lips are feather soft, and his hands are gentle but firm. I should have invited him in. Yes, my parents are upstairs, but so what? It's not like we'd have sex. I reach for the knob. He felt so good and so right.

Right. The word stops me cold. Just like Ward. Just like every guy before Ward. They were all geeks, and they all felt right. Right up until they dumped me for their geeky game obsession or the hotter geek girl across the room.

I finish reaching for the handle, but instead of turning it, I lock the door. There really is something wrong with me. Tonight wasn't even a date. We played M and M with his friends at his friend's place.

But it was real. It brought back everything I loved in college—losing myself in a character, working as a team, having fun. When was the last time I had fun? I've spent so many waking moments worrying about letting my guard down, worrying about letting another Ward into my life. Then I do something I always did with Ward, and it's nowhere near the same. Tonight was great, and Craig made it happen without even realizing it.

I pick my way across the room, careful to check with my feet before stepping. I could just turn on a light like a normal person, but the dark is feeding my comfort. The analogy's been used a million times, but the darkness is a blanket or a cocoon. Instead of warmth, though, it wraps me in belief. As long as it remains dark, as long as I preserve the essence of the last few moments with Craig, I can feel safe in my decisions. If I turn on a light, the cocoon will shatter—because blankets don't shatter—and it's not worth it. Maybe I'll have fear or regret or questions in the morning, but tonight, I'm going to let this be. I'm going to believe that I can be a geek and a girl and have a guy who shares my interests.

And I'm not going to be afraid.

Chapter 13: Craig

I park at Sierra Plaza and get out of my car. Molly is leaning against her black and silver car, looking gorgeous in a light purple dress and heels. Her hair is pulled back, and she's wearing a necklace, the exact details of which escape me at this distance. My hormones go into overdrive, and I have to remind them we aren't going somewhere secluded. Jesus, I've only been away from her for two days, and I'm reacting like this. So screwed.

I weave around the three cars between us and stop beside her. "You look beautiful."

She blushes, which makes her prettier. "Thanks. Shall we?"

I hold out my arm. She takes it, and I lead her to one end of the plaza.

She pulls me to a halt. "Nuclear Fusion Café." Her pink lips form a pout.

She's thoroughly kissable, but it's not happening now. We're not even officially dating. Aside from that, PDAs are worse than PDGs, especially when one person just does them to the other.

"Have you ever been here?"

"No." She points to the sign. "I don't make a point of dining at places named after dangerous atomic activities."

I release her and open the door. "I eat here all the time, and I'm still standing."

She pauses halfway into the restaurant. "You never know. You could drop at any moment."

On that cheerful note, we get in line. When it comes to our turn, I get the Turkey Flare, and she orders the Fusion Explosion. I pay, and we take a table by the windows.

"This place is interesting," she says after a long pause where she looks around as if she's never seen a café before.

"I come here with the gang sometimes." And to be fair, there aren't many places like Fusion. The walls are covered in sound wave patterns, and the lights are shaped like atoms. The sheer scientific gravity of the place has never really occurred to me before. Even the tables and chairs are decorated with pictures of atoms. "Dawn found it."

"Somehow that doesn't surprise me."

We make small talk about our lives over the last few days while we wait. Hers has been full of work and a shopping trip with a friend from work. I wax a little poetic about the freedom between classes and my summer job. Our number is called, and I go up to get our food.

She stares at her sandwich when I set it down. "That's … interesting."

I put mine down and retake my seat. Mine looks like a chicken sandwich that the sun clung to—the effect accomplished with cheese. Hers has banana peppers, black olives, cucumbers, red onions, and mushrooms artfully organized in the pattern of a hydrogen atom. "Welcome to Fusion."

She pokes at the sandwich.

"Try it," I say in a more sympathetic voice. "I wouldn't bring you to a place that regularly poisons its patrons. At least not out of game."

That gets a smile, and she takes a bite. Her eyes widen. "Wow." Thankfully, she's not like Parker. She chews and swallows before saying more. "That's … intense."

I swallow my own mouthful. "Intense good or intense bad?"

She takes another bite and takes her time. "Good," she says before going for the third.

"Trust the shaman," I say. "For he is wise."

She goes still for a fraction of a second, expression completely off guard, before taking another bite. "Right."

What was that? Did I upset her mentioning M and M in public? Hope not, that's kinda the point of today. Just thinking about it gets my pulse going. I eat faster. The sooner we finish, the sooner we can move on. The plan for this date popped into my head on the way home from her house the other night, and two days of waiting have been torture.

"I'm going to run to the bathroom," Molly says when she finishes her sandwich and then goes before I can respond.

I take my last bite and savor it. It's the perfect day to be out. There isn't a cloud in the sky, and the sun is doing its nuclear fusion thing and bringing light. It's the same kind of light that overtook me two nights ago. If I close my eyes and relax, I can still feel Molly against me, and man, that felt awesome. That needs to repeat, possibly today.

As if the memory called her, Molly slides back into her chair. "The bathrooms are labeled protons and electrons."

I laugh a little. "Did you expect anything else from a place called Nuclear Fusion?"

She opens and closes her mouth, but the glimmer is back in her eyes. Whatever threw her off before, the protons and electrons cleared it up. Hip hip hurray for atoms. "I'm ready to go whenever you are."

We gather our trash and toss it. Back outside, I lead her past a nail place, a kitchen supply store, and a bunch of other shops. I'll never understand how Fusion wound up at the opposite end of the plaza from Bob's, but stranger things have happened.

"Bob's Comics Because Bob is an Under-Appreciated Name." Molly halts in front of the store. "Let me guess, some guy named Bob owns this place."

I open the door. "Not sure. If not, I'd assume some guy who feels bad for the name Bob does."

We go inside, and my inner geek rears its head. The smell of fresh comic books surrounds me as if I am a lion and it fresh wildebeest. The entrancing call of the Serengeti goods speaks to my primal senses. I am a geek in a geek store, and there is little that can distract me from the hunt.

"Whoa," Molly says, breaking the spell a bit. "This is … unique."

I retreat into myself and away from the geek hive mind. "Have you never been to a hobby shop?"

She goes still. Then she shrugs, but the motion is almost unintentional. "Not one like this."

Aren't most geek stores like this? I take a hypothetical step back and try to view Bob's through a newcomer's eyes. Posters for Marvel, DC, and various other comics' characters adorn every millimeter of available wall space. Mobiles made of gaming cards hang from the ceiling, which is painted with superhero logos. The carpet, though, is probably the clincher. Pi starts at one end, and the entire floor is numbers. I make a mental note to show Molly the ellipsis in the back corner and move to stand beside a rack of TARDIS name key chains.

"Bob's is definitely a special place."

"So I see." She inspects a similar group of key chains that are shaped like DNA helixes. "There's just so much."

That's my cue. I take her arm and lead her farther into the store. "Allow me to introduce you."

My primal senses turn into teaching instincts. Molly is my hatchling, and it is my natural duty to educate her in the ways of our kind. The comic books are first—everything from Spiderman to Sweet Tooth. I lead her away from My Little Pony and toward the mana of the truly experienced. Her eyes light up with the fascination of the newly converted. She is coming into her own, growing into an adult geek little by little. There is yet hope for the future.

When we've exhausted the comics, we move to the figurines. There is an entire wall of them, and they range from tiny dragons to foot-long statues.

She comes to one of a wizard and a dragon playing chess, and her entire face practically glows. "That is one of the coolest things I've ever seen."

I have to agree. "Expensive, but awesome. When I'm independently wealthy, that's the first one I buy for my collection."

To her credit, she doesn't look at me like I'm nuts. "Good to have well-aligned priorities." Ah, good, she begins to understand.

We finish up with the figurines, ooh-ing and ah-ing over a few more. Next are card games. Yu-Gi-Oh, Magic the Gathering, and Pokémon, among others, leer at us from their tiny plastic packets. Growls, sword strikes, and howls show their bloodlust. They want us to set them free. We are strong, though. We don't give in. This is a learning time. Further pursuits may come later. For now, this is about comfort. Molly's given no sign of divulging the reason for what seems to be a fear of geek, but I'm determined to break her of it. Fear ultimately leads to suffering—a lesson or two in condensing would have done the Jedi good.

Either way, there's no suffering here. The longer we stay in the store, the less tense her shoulders become. She moves from one display to the next like a kid seeing flowers for the first time. There's a tender curiosity in every movement. Her walls are coming down.

Warmth gathers in my chest. She's at ease, and I'm at least partially responsible for it. That rocks my world in a way I didn't think possible. I've never wanted anyone to feel comfortable as much as I want her to now.

"I can't believe I've never been to a store like this," she says as she replaces a box of dice.

"Me neither." I wrap my arm around her waist and pull her to my side.

She rests her head on my shoulder. For a moment, we're quiet and still. There's no need to explore, no need to speak. There's a mutual understanding here. This is a life we both want, crave. I've lived it forever. She's tried to suppress it, but there's no suppressing the siren call of geekdom. Its claws are stronger than those of a velociraptor, and once they grab hold, they never let go.

"Thanks," she says after a long silence. She pulls free and wanders around the display to check out the next.

I stay and just watch. If she didn't already, this girl's got a piece of my heart, and I have no regrets.

Someone punches my shoulder. "Craig, you mother, I haven't seen you in forever."

The manly geek side of me slams to the forefront of my mind with a crash. Holy crap, I haven't seen this guy in forever—at least high school. This is turning out to be a pretty awesome day. And even better, I can introduce Molly to some more geeks.

I turn and punch the guy's shoulder. "How you been, Ward?"

Chapter 14: Molly

Ward. Ward is less than ten feet away. The walking-on-a-rainbow feeling falls away, and gravity takes over. I plunge back to Earth, disoriented. What is he doing here? Why isn't he in some geek store up where he lives?

And if his presence isn't bad enough, somehow, he knows Craig.

I duck around the display and into the next aisle. I can't let him see me. He and Craig are chatting it up like they've known each other for years—maybe they have. What if Ward sees me and starts bad-mouthing me to Craig? What if Craig listens, or worse, agrees? Get a grip, Molls. Craig isn't like that. He won't turn on me because of something Ward says.

But what if he does? God, I'm so stupid. Why did I agree to come out today? Why did I let him pick the place? Why did I walk into this store? It's a geek store. Nothing good ever comes from hanging out in geek stores.

"We're playing Chanter's back there," Ward says. I'm-just-so-cool-because-I-play-this-game drips from every word. He hasn't changed at all. "Wanna join us?"

I inch down the aisle and peek through the gaps between

displays. Ward's appearance hasn't changed either. He's wearing one of his signature *Star Wars* T-shirts, and his black hair is flat against his head. It practically glitters from all the mousse. I can't believe I used to run my fingers through that. Phantom slime coats my hands, and a shiver wracks my body.

Craig shrugs and puts his hands in his pockets. "Thanks, but no thanks. I don't have a deck." That's his excuse? "And even if I did, I'm here with someone."

No, go back to not having a deck. Forget that you're here with me. Use not having a deck as the excuse.

"Oh?" Ward says. "Who?"

I pull back behind the shelves so fast I get whiplash. My heart races, and I put a hand to my chest. Don't say my name. Whatever you do, don't say my name.

"A girl," Craig says.

I could kiss him.

"Though," he says. "She might wanna check it out."

Or not.

"Oh?" Ward's tone is the kind that comes with his signature eyebrow raise. "A geeky girl? She hot?"

I start to cover my ears but can't bring myself to stop listening. As shallow as it is, I want to hear the answer.

"She's pretty," Craig says. "Really pretty." His voice goes soft as if pretty isn't the right word.

My heart melts a little. Maybe this won't be a disaster.

"But not hot?" Ward snorts. "C'mon, man, you're doin' it wrong if she's not offering you anything in return for being as geeky as you. Bring her back, and I'll let you know if she's worth keeping." His footsteps pad over the carpet until a door opens and closes.

I straighten and lower my hand. What a jerk. What an

absolute, total, complete—

"Molly?" Craig rounds the display at the end of the aisle. His eyes find me, and he goes a little pale. "Hey, you all right?" He's at my side, supporting me with an arm around my waist.

I brush off his concern. "I'm fine. My heels are just killing me." It's as good a lie as any.

"Oh." His color returns. "I'm not sure if you heard, but I ran into a friend. They're playing Chanter's Fray in the back, if you wanna check it out."

"No." I said that way too fast. I cough and offer him a smile. "No, thanks. I think I need to go take off these shoes."

"You can do that out back," he says. "And sit. Come on, it'll be—"

"No." It's a struggle, but I force my voice to come out calm. "Really. I just need to go home, take off the shoes, and sit in the quiet." I brush my hand over my forehead. "A headache is coming on."

"Oh." His face falls, but it's impossible to tell if it's over me cutting our day short or because he feels bad for my fake headache. "Are you sure? I can get you some meds or something."

I am now. "Yes." He's more upset about missing the game than he is about me leaving. His insistence to find a way to keep me here confirms it.

To his credit, he wipes the disappointment away. "I'll go tell my friend I can't stay. I can make sure you get home safe."

Oh hell, no. I don't need or want him following me now. If he comes with me, he'll just complain about not being able to stay and play his little boy games. "That's okay." I pull out of his arm and put some distance between us. "I'll be fine, really. Go have fun." Fun comes out harsh. I can't help it.

He blinks, slow. "Molly, I—"

"Don't worry about it." I back to the end of the aisle. "I'll see you later." That's vague enough. Later could mean tomorrow or never.

He hesitates. It's the moment of truth. The Craig I think I know will offer to come with me anyway. The Craig who knows Ward will go play. Simple—geeky guys always are.

"Okay." He moves toward the back of the store. Guess he's a Ward type. "I'll call you later. Take it easy." There's real regret and concern in his voice, but he's still choosing the game over me.

"Yeah." Tears prick at the back of my eyes like mini arrows. Why am I crying? I'm angry, not sad. I need to go before he suspects. "Bye."

I all but stagger through and out of the store. Ten steps at a dead run in heels—beat that, Croft—see me at Dessy. I expect the tears to flash flood as soon as I'm in the car, but they don't. Maybe I really am getting over Ward.

And maybe I will have to get over Craig before we even start. It's not fair. We had something the other night. That kiss was real. I want it to be real, but it can't be. He knows Ward. All of Ward's guy friends are jerks. Why should Craig be any different?

I start Dessy and drive toward home. Five minutes into the ride, the silence becomes too much, and I turn on the radio. Appropriately, Black Keys is rocking about a two-faced significant other. It's the kind of emotional precision only found with a natural twenty bluff roll, and I crank the volume up until Dessy's frame shakes. I should probably feel more concerned about making a car named Desdemona uncomfortable or angry, but I can't make myself care. I need something to be louder than my thoughts.

I turn onto the highway and roll the windows down. The wind on my face and in my hair cleanses my emotions. This is power. This is freedom—cruising at seventy miles per hour and feeling the bass in my bones. It was the cure-all after breaking up with Ward. How fitting that it works for sort of breaking up with the guy who knows Ward.

I get off the highway and turn the music down. It's amazing what breaking a speed limit and disturbing the peace will do for an outlook on life. Nothing can stop this high.

My text noise goes off.

Craig? My heart gives a hopeful thump, and my palms go sweaty. What is wrong with me? I don't want to talk to him. I don't want the guy who will come chasing after me on a guilt trip. If it's him, I won't respond.

Lucky for me, it's not him. It's Nikki asking if I'm free. She's off work and bored.

I text back a *ya*—the least amount of letters to answer because texting and driving is a bad idea—and drop my phone. Her response to meet her at Crest's comes right away. I text *k*—look at me outdoing myself after *ya*—and change course.

Five minutes later, I park next to Nikki's red sports car. She is a way better twenty-something than me. She waves when I enter the coffee shop. I wave back and get in line. The place calms me. The lack of people is partly responsible, but it's more the lack of geeky design. Here I'm just a normal girl that no one will suspect of playing Lords or liking a guy who plays M and M.

The line moves fast. Three people and too many dollars later, I take my mochaccino and join Nikki at a table by the windows. "How goes it?"

"I need to quit A's," she says.

I sip my coffee and instantly regret it. The scalding liquid sets my mouth on fire more effectively than a red dragon. "You always say that after a rough shift."

She waves a hand. "I know. But this time I mean it."

We exchange a glance and shrug, both knowing she's not quitting any time soon.

"So," she says after a sip of her coffee. "You got here fast."

I stare into my mug. "I was out."

"Oh? Where?"

I shift my cup, but it doesn't magically reveal whether I should tell the truth or not. Then again, this is Nikki. She'll find out somehow. "With Craig."

"And you left?" She raises her eyebrows. "You had that hunk alone, and you took off? Girl, what is the matter with you?"

I take another careful sip. They say heat doesn't hurt as much when you're prepared. Whoever they are, they lie. They also say honesty is the best policy, but I don't want to talk about this. I'm not ready to talk about this. "He ran into someone and had to go."

Nikki clucks her tongue. "Too bad. He's a hot one."

"Is that all you care about?" My voice comes out angry. "How hot he is?"

Nikki shrugs. "It's a factor." She pats my hand where it rests on the table. "Seriously, Molls, if he just up and leaves like that without a good reason, be careful. It might not work out."

"I know." And that's the trouble. I do know. I've been through it before.

The memory of the kiss won't let go, though. It felt more right than Ward ever did. There was caring and trust and desire in that kiss. I don't want to lose a chance with him, but

I'm not willing to date another guy who ditches me for a game he'll spend the rest of the night playing as if I don't exist.

Chapter 15: Craig

I'm leaving. I don't even know why I agreed to stay. Even if I hadn't lost the last two games, my heart isn't here. It's with Molly's dejected expression. I'm such a moron.

But she'd told me to stay. She'd all but yelled at me, and she'd given off the I-wanna-be-alone vibe pretty strongly. I didn't run after her or text her for that reason, and I'm starting to think I made a mistake.

"Demonplain to Craig." Ward waves a hand in front of my face. "You there?"

I swat his hand away. Definitely made a mistake. "Yeah, but not for much longer." I gather the cards and put them back in their box. "I'm gonna head out. Thanks for the games."

"Aww, sore loser?" Ward grins. "C'mon, one more go."

I close the box. Even if I was gonna play another round, it wouldn't be with this deck. It's silver with control and deck-destruction mechanics, and it's not working for me. I don't even like silver. Ward's playing black/red—red fire spells and black deck-replenish—which makes the deck-destruction freaking useless. There's a list of more fun things I could be doing right now, and most of the items at its top involve Molly. Being eaten by a Cyclops isn't far behind.

"Not sore," I say. "Just gotta go."

Ward gives me a mock pout. "It's okay, man. I understand. I hate losing too."

Wow, he's changed. I really don't remember him being this much of a jerk. "Think what you want." I stand and cross to the door. "I'll see you around."

"Speaking of that." Ward leans back in his chair. "I'm not doing anything tomorrow. We should terrorize this pathetic town."

My stomach lurches. Why does spending time with Ward feel like diving headfirst into a cauldron of bubbling chimera fat? Facing that tarrasque doesn't sound so bad by comparison. I don't want to match his level of jerk-ness, though. "Sure."

He slides his phone out of his pocket. "Number?"

I give it. He texts me, and I save his to my phone.

"Just like the old days." He splits his cards into two piles and starts to shuffle. "Later, bro."

"Later." I'm out of the store faster than the Flash. In the car, I stare at my phone. Part of me wants to text Molly. Another part says texting her is a bad idea. She left in a huff and was adamant that I don't follow. That's a signal for space, and what kind of needy jerk would I be if I intruded on that?

I start the car and just drive. Sometimes having no destination is the way to go. The early summer breeze is mana for my wounded heart. Why did she tell me to get lost? Did she not want me around? I need a distraction. I need to be around people.

As if in response to my realization, my phone buzzes for an incoming call, and Lyd's name pops up. My hands shake as I reach for the phone. If she's holding another guy off Amber, I'm gonna lose it. "Hey, Lyd."

"Hey, you busy?" That's a good sign. She wouldn't have started with that if it was about my sister.

"Not really." Never mind that I should be. "What's up?"

There's a pause and a thunk on the other end of the line. "Do you wanna help me move furniture? I got a new bookshelf. Randy was here, but he got called into work."

I turn right instead of left at the next intersection. Randy is the best brother Lyd could ask for, but he works with special needs kids. When work calls, work calls. "Sure, I'll be right there." I hang up and navigate to Lyd's house.

She meets me at the front door. For once, her hair is down. It falls past her shoulders and does flattering things for her heart-shaped face. It's similar to how Molly wears her hair, and the rejection pain flares again.

I push it away and follow Lyd inside. It's not fair to pine about the girl I wanna date while I'm hanging out with my best friend, who happens to be a girl. "So where is this shelf?"

Lyd leads me into her room. Her old bookshelf is in its usual spot, and the replacement version leans against her bed.

"I see where that might be a problem."

She crosses to the old shelf and grabs a stack of books. "I have no idea when Randy will be back, and I kind of want to sleep tonight."

"Don't blame you." I help her move the books. When the three levels of the old shelf are empty, we lug it, awkwardly due to the way Lyd's house is set up, out to the living room. "What do you want to do with this thing?"

She points to an empty corner. "We can leave it there for now. I think Randy knows someone who needs it."

"That works." We place it in said corner and wander back to Lyd's room. There, I grab the new shelf and thank whoever's listening that I know how to lift. It weighs a ton. "This is a solid piece." I knock on its side.

Lyd takes the other end. "I'm glad the soon-to-be-expert approves."

"Just call me Carpenter Craig." I wince. "Actually, don't call me that."

"Don't worry. I won't. Probably."

We stand the shelf up and slide it into the old one's place. It's four levels instead of three, but the extra height doesn't make the room look smaller. I help her reorganize her collection, and there's room to spare when we're done, which I assume was the point

"Ta-da," Lyd says, throwing her arms wide and flopping back on the bed. "Thanks for the use of your muscles."

I flex, and she giggles. When was the last time she and I just hung out? Forget that, when was the last time I was at her house? Not that much has changed. Her bedroom walls are still a light purple. The curtains and bedspread are a darker purple, and her dresser still boasts about a zillion dragon statues. Yup, that's Lyd.

"I feel like I haven't seen you in forever," Lyd says after a short silence.

Great minds think alike. "Probably because we haven't seen each other in a while. Not outside of M and M, anyway."

"Great minds think alike." It's a little scary that she says my thoughts out loud. She sits up. "Wanna see a movie?"

I check my phone. It's only three o'clock? Molly really did cut out early. The thought of her name gets that nagging voice in my head going again. It tells me to call her. I ignore it. Molly wants to be left alone, and I owe Lyd some hangout time. "Sure."

Lyd scrambles off the bed and sits at her desk. "Now to find a movie worth seeing."

Twenty minutes and a bunch of terrible options later, we decide on the latest from the X-Men franchise. Lyd and I pile into my car and spend the next two hours in badass heaven. Seriously, Wolverine is one of my favorites, and what isn't cool about having an adamantium-plated skeleton? So the process of getting it wasn't so great. It's metal-plated bones.

"I'm hungry," Lyd says when we step out of the theater. "Watching Hugh Jackman beat things up is a lot of work."

I poke her side. "And that giant popcorn didn't help any?"

She links her arm through mine and drags me toward the food court. "Popcorn is not food, you poor, unfortunate soul."

Pizza apparently meets Ursula's requirements, though. We each order two slices and find a table. The place is a zoo with kids running and screaming and parents running and screaming after their kids. The food court designers anticipated this, however. At least, it seems like they did. Lyd and I take one of the alcove tables. They afford a level of privacy and allow conversations to be carried on where both participants can hear.

"Thanks for hanging out," Lyd says between bites.

I chug a decent amount of my soda and shrug. "No problem." My attempt at a lighthearted tone falls flatter than a two-sided die. "I was just driving around aimlessly before you called me."

"Something wrong?" She knows me too well.

The question is, what do I tell her? I'm told talking about potential girlfriends with female friends is always awkward, but Lyd isn't just a random female friend. We've known each other since before we could talk.

"Well, well, if it isn't the sore loser." Or maybe Ward will show up and end the conversation. He stops beside our table and swipes my uneaten crust, shoving it in his mouth.

I glare at him. "Have you heard of asking before taking food?"

Ward shrugs one shoulder. "Touchy. Take a pill." He says all of that with his mouth full. That's not cool when Parker does it, but it's even less okay with Ward. Thankfully, he swallows before speaking again. "What brings you to the mall? I thought you had a hot date?" His gaze goes to Lyd, and a twisted grin overtakes his features. "Oh, never mind. I guess you do have a hot date." He holds out a hand. "Ward."

My protective instincts rear. Why is he acting like he doesn't know her? Oh, right, because he doesn't. Lyd never joined that game group, and if this is what at least one of those guys grew into, I'm glad.

Lyd doesn't need protection, though. She squares her shoulders and levels him with a look she must have learned from Dawn. "Lydia," she says, not taking his hand. The message is clear—*lecherous creep, leave me alone.*

"A pleasure to meet you." Ward shoves his hands in his pockets. "More than you know. Well, don't let me keep you lovebirds. Later." He swaggers away.

When he's out of earshot—three feet away with mall noise—I let out a breath. "Sorry about that."

Lyd adjusts to a more comfortable position. "Who is he?"

"Some guy I used to game with." I shake my head. "He's always been kind of like that."

Lyd rolls her eyes. "If *by that,* you mean he's the dickiest dick who ever dicked …."

I almost choke, and we collapse into hysterics. Everything that went wrong today fades to the background. I needed this time out, bad. Tomorrow, I can fix things with Molly. Funny that I needed to hang with a girl to get over my issues with another girl.

We finish our pizza in record time and take our leave, managing to only have one group of kids run in front of us.

"Well, I think I've satisfied my mandatory mall time quota for the next ten years," Lyd says when we're in the parking lot.

I beep my car open and get her door. "Only ten?"

She responds by getting into the car and giving the mall the bird.

That works. I go around to my side, get in, and start the car. Then I sit and wait while five cars, which weren't there a minute ago, drive past me. When the parade is over, I back out before the next one can start and take the path of least resistance to the main road.

"Thanks." Lyd doesn't look at me, but her voice is full of some emotion I can't name.

I turn down the street that leads to her neighborhood. "Anytime. I'm a pro with furniture, remember?"

She laughs, quiet. "Not that. Though, thanks for that too. I meant hanging out tonight. I needed to get out."

I can't respond. When did we get to the point in our lives that we need to thank each other for spending time? Have I been that busy since school let out? I'm going to have to do something about that. My friendship with Lyd is more important than one night out. "Anytime for that too. You know that."

She hums and falls silent.

I open and close my mouth for a minute, but no good conversation starters come. Guess Lyd's got the right idea. The rest of the ride consists of her staring out the window and me driving. At her house, I park at the curb and go around to get her door.

"I had fun," I say when we're on the sidewalk.

"Me too." She's still quiet, and now her expression is distant.

Oh hell, no. Clearly, she doesn't want to talk, and I'm not going to force her. But my best friend isn't allowed to look like her favorite bow broke on my watch, especially when I might be part of the cause. I close the distance between us and catch her in a bone-crushing hug. She sucks in a breath and squirms, but I don't let go. I've never seen anyone need a hug this much.

The pointless struggling continues for another second before she gives up and wraps her arms around my neck. She rests her head on my shoulder, and every big brother instinct I have kicks into overdrive. There's defeat in the way she moves, the way she breathes. Someone's hurt her recently, and I haven't been there. Well, that changes, now.

"You okay?"

She breathes, deep, and seems to knit back together. "Fine." Her voice is stronger.

I squeeze her and let go, and she lowers her arms and steps back. As hoped, the hug did her wonders. She's standing straighter and actually smiling.

"Thanks for that." She pats my shoulder. "I'm gonna head in. So I'll see you when I see you."

"Which will be soon. Promise."

She nods and starts up the walkway.

I wait until she has the front door open before getting in my car and starting the engine. She turns back, and I wave.

She responds with the live long and prosper sign.

And that's why we're best friends.

A few streets later, I'm home. For once, Dad's car is here on a Saturday night—a regular miracle. I let myself into the house.

The downstairs is dead silent, and the someone-is-coming-home-late light is on. I kill it and climb the stairs. This has, without a doubt, been one of the weirdest days I've had in a while. There are so many mixed feelings, but at least it's ending on a positive note. Things can be fixed.

I take the last step, brushing my hand against the railing. Something stings and slides into my hand.

I suck in a breath and grunt. What the ... a splinter? There shouldn't be splinters in this railing. It's smooth wood. Nevertheless, there is a piece of wood in my hand. I poke it, because apparently I've forgotten every rule about splinters, and it goes a bit farther in. K, no more touching the splinter. Get the tweezers, except the bathroom door is closed.

It opens, and Amber pokes her head out. "Craig? You okay?"

I hold up my hand. "Splinter. I need the tweezers."

She opens the door and motions for me to come in. I do, and she pulls the tweezers out of a drawer.

"Where is it?"

"My finger." I show her.

She bites her lip. "How did you ... it's way in there." She grabs my hand and holds it still. "Don't move." She digs into my skin.

I make some undignified, distinctly high-pitched noise.

"I'm sorry." She pokes me again. "I've almost got it." Another minute of prodding, and the sliver slides out.

I tap the hole. It stings. "All that for a tiny piece of wood?"

Amber gets the alcohol out of the medicine cabinet. "Yeah." She sterilizes the tweezers and pours some good old H2O2 on my hand. "You might consider a Band-Aid."

I do more than consider. I don't want to get alcohol all over everything. "Did I interrupt you?"

She waves a hand. "No. I was just going to bed. I have an early morning."

That's right. She does. And here's someone else I haven't paid enough attention to lately. This day just keeps getting weirder. "Sorry about that. Don't let me keep you."

"It's fine." She washes her hands and scoots past me. "See you tomorrow."

"Night," I say.

Her bedroom door closes. I take the opportunity to use the bathroom and then hunker in my own room. Did the world flip upside down and not tell me? Amber's being nice. Lyd was upset.

Molly ….

I clamp down on the urge to blame myself before it consumes me. I'll deal with it tomorrow. It will be okay. For now, though, my sister has the right idea. An early morning and a brand new start are the way to go.

Chapter 16: Molly

I deliver a salad and a cucumber and avocado sandwich—eww—to the couple seated in the private corner table at A's. They barely look up from ogling each other to thank me.

"Do you need anything else?"

They answer by shaking their heads, still not looking away from each other, and I make my retreat, heart aching. It's not that I want a guy to stare at me and ignore the rest of the world. Just having a guy who actually wanted me around would be nice.

"Keep it up and you'll make enough in tips to go to Disney," Nikki says as she passes me on her way out of the kitchen. "Energizer bunny."

I offer her a grin and skip to the counter to grab the next order. Doing everything in speed mode helps me not think about Craig and how he just ditched me like I didn't matter even though I'm pretty sure I looked pathetic and like I wanted him to chase after me and not go play stupid games with stupid Ward.

Or maybe speed mode doesn't help. Why do I still think he cares? It's been twenty-four hours, and he hasn't called or texted. Then again, I did tell him to leave me alone, but that was only supposed to be short term. I didn't want him to really leave me alone. Not that he knew the difference, but he should have known. Guys are supposed to know this stuff.

Wow, that is the absolute dumbest thing I have ever thought in my life. How is he supposed to know this stuff? Despite all the games he plays, he does not actually have the ability to read minds. That skill does not exist in the real world, and expecting him to know what I'm thinking because I saw Ward and was upset … classy, not. Bottom line: If it's going to happen, it'll happen, and if it doesn't, I'll put Craig and Ward behind me and meet a perfectly undorky guy to go on perfectly undorky dates with. Alakazam, done.

I grab the burgers for my other table and scoot out of the kitchen. A group waits by the host's desk, and the host is nowhere to be seen. If they're still there after I deliver this order, I'll take care of them. The burgers go to a couple of high school girls. They thank me and politely say no when I ask if there's anything else they need. Where were those kinds of girls when I was in high school? I turn to head back to the kitchen, and make eye contact with Ward.

The floor goes out from under me, and the bottomless pit swallows me whole. What is he doing here? Does he know I work here? Well, he does now, but is that why he came? To stalk me? I claw my way out of the pit and race through the labyrinth of tables back to the safe chamber of the kitchen. It's a recall point. The monsters in the dungeon can't reach me here. It's gonna take more than a quick rest to regen all the health I just lost, though.

"Hey, Molls." And Nikki is going to be of no help. "Craig is here." Her voice is flirty. Has she forgotten what happened yesterday? Does she not realize that Ward is here and that Ward is more of a problem than Craig?

Of course she doesn't. She doesn't even know Ward.

"Is he alone?"

"No," Nikki says, the flirtiness gone. "He's with a group, and they're at one of your tables."

Of course he is. Why would he come alone, unless he was here to see me, which he's not because he's with people. "Guess I better do my job, then." I grab the water pitcher off the counter. Life can be cruel. Why is he always at one of my tables? I need to have a word with the host about that, but I'll do that later. Right now, Craig is a distraction, if a bad one, from Ward. I march to the door, prepping my shields. Nothing is going to touch me today. Three more steps, all systems go. Two, one.

Craig is with Ward.

I jump back and lose my grip on the pitcher. It hits the floor, and thank the pantheon it's only a quarter full.

"Molly?" Nikki is at my side, somehow not slipping in the puddle. "What happened? Are you okay?"

Okay. It takes me a minute to remember what the word means. I can't process anything but Craig. It's a fight to push him to the background. I'm not strong enough for this, but it needs to be done. Slowly, one agonizing millimeter at a time, I make progress, and the rest of the world comes back into focus. I start to take a deep breath but don't make it. Craig is here with Ward. That takes every iota of energy I have, and I shatter into a billion pieces. A choked, broken sound escapes my lips. Okay? I'm nothing like okay. This can't be happening.

But it is. "He's with Ward."

"Ward?" Nikki's voice shoots up about an octave. "You're

jerk-face ex-boyfriend Ward? He's here? And who's with him?"

"Craig." His name comes as three syllables because my body is shaking so hard. "They know each other." And the truth about yesterday comes out. I should have known better than to withhold in the first place. Crest's would have been a much better place to tell this story.

When I'm done, Nikki wraps her arm around my shoulders. "K, I'm taking that table. Even if he is here to see you, he doesn't deserve to now. Sit down for a minute."

I wipe my hand across my forehead. "He might not know about Ward and me. I didn't tell him." But Ward might have talked about his ex-girlfriend, and Craig's not stupid. He'll have put two and two together.

"Doesn't matter." Nikki redoes her ponytail and rearranges her chest to make the most of her push-up bra. "Now sit while I take care of this." She struts out of the kitchen like a vengeful blonde cockatrice.

I pick up the pitcher and sit as instructed. The plastic is clammy in my clammy hands, and everything shudders. What am I doing? It's my table, and I'm not this wimpy. I should be able to take care of this. What kind of message am I sending Ward by staying in the kitchen and letting Nikki fight my battles for me? It's not that I'm over him, that's for sure, and that's the problem. I want to be over him. He shouldn't have this kind of hold on me.

Well, there are other places to go besides Ward's table. I drop the pitcher in the dirty dishes area and head for the bathrooms, using A's maze setup to my advantage. It's cowardly, but Nikki will give a full report. I check with my other two tables—both are doing fine—and make it to the bathroom without incident. Cool water on my face and a few minutes later, I feel more human. I take the deep breath that escaped me, completing my transformation, and dry off. I'm ready. Now to find Nikki and reclaim my table. I leave the bathroom, plaster a smile on my face, and come face-to-face with Ward.

His eyes light up like a Christmas tree on steroids, and if that's not bad enough, there's no surprise in them. He knew I worked here. He came here on purpose. "Well, well, if it isn't my ex-girlfriend. How you been?" His voice is a continuous line of smarm. "I had a feeling you were the person Craig was here to see. Pity he doesn't know about you."

I swallow, hard, and my carefully reconstructed defenses start to crumble. Stupid, stupid, stupid move, leaving the kitchen. Now I'm trapped, and there's no Nikki to come to my rescue. "He's not here to see me, and even if he is, I don't want to know him if he's friends with you." I'm not sure how I get all that out, but I do.

Ward puts his hand to his heart, his face a mask of mock pain. "Oh, those words hurt. Not like it hurt when you said we were over, though. And for someone who's only had one or two conversations with the guy, you spend an awful lot of time with him at places like Bob's, for example."

The bottomless pit swallows me again, but there's no climbing out this time. He saw me at Bob's? But I stayed out of sight. I purposefully stayed out of his line of sight. The world fragments. I'm going to break all over again, and Ward's blocking my only real exit. If I retreat into the bathroom, he'll just wait for me to come out. He's done it before.

"Yeah, I was going to tell you the other day, but you left." Ward leans forward, getting into my space. "Be careful around Craig. I mean, you never know when a guy has another girl in the wings. Just thought I'd let you know so you can cut it off before you get too emotionally invested. You and your emotions." He runs his gaze up my body and then goes into the men's room.

I sag back against the wall, my legs threatening to give. Oh my god, what a prick. What a no-good jerk. He still says stuff he knows will hurt, and he still knows how to make me feel worthless. And the worst part is, I'm second-guessing. Does Craig have another girl? Was he setting me up to fall? What does he really think of me? Tears gather. I wipe them away and breathe. I can't go out there like this, but I can't stay put either. It will only get worse if I'm still here when Ward comes out of the bathroom.

That makes my decision. I wipe away a second batch of tears and poke my head around the corner. No one's coming, and most of the customers are intent on their meals and company. Head down, I make my escape, taking an indirect but little-populated route. The few people I pass don't flag me for anything, and no one seems to notice that I'm barely holding it together. So far so good, I'm in the clear. I'm rolling twenties for stealth. It's only another ten feet. I'm going to make it. I look up to calculate my next move.

And there's Craig.

Our eyes lock. He smiles, and then his eyes go dark. *Are you all right?* He mouths the words.

No. No, I'm not. I turn away and bolt for the kitchen. Screw the twenties for stealth. Speed is my friend. I burst into the kitchen, entire body shaking now. "I'm taking my break," I say to anyone in earshot and dash out the back door. The alley behind A's is blissfully empty. I make a beeline—who actually took the time to watch bees flying back to the hive, anyway—to Dessy, beep her open, and curl up in the backseat.

Away from people, Niagara Falls rains from my eyes. It's not a pretty cry either. It's an all-out snotfest. Gross. I dig out the pack of tissues I keep in the compartment between the front seats. It's tiny and useless, and I'm convinced the same person who named beeline thought that ten flimsy tissues were enough for a broken heart. That person obviously lived a very happy life and failed geometry.

Geometry, math. I met Ward in my college math class. The tears triple—Niagara Falls during a hurricane. I'm never dating again. All guys want from me is someone to have on their arm and boss around. They figure if nothing else presents itself in a week, they can fall back on me. Then when something hotter and just as reliable shows up, they ditch me. Well, no more. I'm done. No more.

There's a knock on the window.

Against every instinct telling me to ignore it, I look up through a haze of tears and then immediately wish I hadn't.

It's Craig.

Chapter 17: Craig

"Molly? Molly, what happened?" What's going on? I've never seen anyone cry like this. I reach for the back door handle, and she slams the lock into place. Something's hit her, hard, and whatever it is, she doesn't want me to help.

That stings like a bite from a giant spider, and I lower my hand. Did I cause this? How? "Molly, come on, talk to me." I know she can hear me. Car windows aren't that thick. "Please, you're killing me."

That gets a reaction. Her shoulders stop shaking for a second before starting again, less violently. She blows her nose and lifts her head. The raw hurt isn't in her eyes anymore—thank God—but there isn't relief either. She slides across the seat and gets out the other rear door.

"Killing you?" She doesn't scream, but the words hit me like an ogre's club anyway. "I'm killing you. Well, isn't that wonderful for me. That makes it all better, knowing you're in pain. Thank you for coming all the way out here to tell me that."

What? "Molly, what are you talking about? I—"

"What am I talking about? Hmm, let's see." She strides

around the back of the car and stops inches from me. Her cherry scent fills my nose. I ignore it.

"I can't undo damage," she says, her voice more under control. "So I'll just clear up a few things. I'm not here to be your personal punching bag, and I'm not jealous and overbearing. I'm a normal person, and normal people get upset when their significant others cheat on them. Now, if you'll excuse me." She starts to elbow past me.

"Whoa, stop." I put out my arm to hold her back. "Where did this come from? I wasn't aware we were officially anything, and I don't think you're overbearing or jealous at all. And why would I use you as a punching bag?"

She freezes halfway to another shove. Our eyes meet, and there's hope and a silent prayer in her gaze. She wants to believe me.

She should believe me. I'm telling the truth. Why is she accusing me of all this without a reason or anything to back it up? "Where did you get those thoughts? What makes you think I'm only interested in using you somehow?"

She doesn't answer, and the silence weighs a million pounds. Part of me wants to take her in my arms until the pain goes away, but another part—the larger part—doesn't want to touch her until this is sorted out. More-than-friends is on the table for whatever we have, but not if she's going to randomly accuse me of things that haven't been an issue. We stare at each other for a long moment. There's hurt in her eyes, but there's fear and anger too. Fear and anger about what, though?

Finally, she shakes her head. "I have to get back to work."

Apparently I'm not gonna get an answer. "Fine." I step aside so she can pass.

She all but runs back across the parking lot. I tell myself I'm not going to watch her go, but that's a lie. The smaller part of me now wants to run after her, but there's no way. Not now. She couldn't even answer a simple question, and this is, as far as I can tell, a non-issue. How would she react to Amber? Clearly, she's insecure about something. If she can't handle this, she'll never handle me needing to take time out of a relationship to babysit my sister, who's old enough to babysit herself.

Unless it's not insecurity. Is this about being geeky? Is this all a front because she really doesn't want to be seen dating a guy like me? Even if it is, that doesn't excuse her behavior. There are less painful ways to deliver that message.

I trudge back to the main entrance of the restaurant. Standing in the parking lot isn't going to get me answers, and I left my friends hanging. Inside, I plaster a smile on my face and march back to my table.

Parker's gone, probably getting himself into whatever he gets himself into. Ward is back from the bathroom and moving in on Sonya, who keeps scooting away from him.

"Hey, what did I miss?" I plop into my chair.

Ward stops trying to look down Sonya's shirt. "Nothing. Parker had to take a dump." Wow, how eloquent. "And we were getting to know each other."

Sonya glares plus five daggers of fire at him and pulls her hair over her shoulder. "Are you all right, Craig? You ran out of here like a mob of rabid kobolds were on your tail."

I shrug. I'm not about to bring up the thing with Molly. I don't wanna hear about how I made a mistake because I'm not sure I did, not yet. Plus, it's none of Sonya's or Ward's business. "I forgot my phone in the car, and I'm waiting for a call."

"Oh," Sonya says.

Ward rubs his hands together. "I hope you didn't miss the call." He puts emphasis on the last three words.

I pat my pocket. I got it all right, and it went terribly. "Nope."

Parker comes back, and a few minutes later, Nikki brings our food out. Ward entertains us by giving play-by-play descriptions of all the people he's wasted at card games lately. He even uses those exact words. Sonya rolls her eyes so much they might as well be D20s, and Parker and I exchange looks that say so many things, none of them complimentary. Fifteen minutes later, we pay the bill—for which Ward was five bucks short—and regroup outside.

"You guys wanna come to Bob's?" Ward says. "I'm gonna beast this afternoon." Seriously, where does he get his vocabulary?

Sonya lets out a snort that she turns into a cough. "Sounds like a blast, but I have to go. Appointment to get my left third eyelash amputated, has to be booked months in advance. You understand." She scurries to her car.

"Girls," Ward says after she drives away. "They shouldn't play anyway. What about you two bumbholes?"

"I greatly dislike being likened to that part of the anatomy," Parker says.

It's my turn to turn something into a cough, though it's a laugh. Parker's language can be as messed up as Ward's, but at least his is funny.

Ward shrugs. "No big. It's every Saturday. I'll see you guys later. Good luck with the call, Craig." He emphasizes *call* again and heads to his car.

"I also dislike him," Parker says when Ward is gone.

"I'm starting to, too," I say. "He's not the same guy I knew in high school."

"Polymorph spells will do that." Parker points to the lot. "Shall we depart?"

I pull out my keys. Departing sounds excellent. I'm done with A's for a while, and standing in front of it only reminds me of Molly, which only causes me pain. "Let's go."

We pile into my car and use the drive to discuss what we want when we reach level three in the game. I drop Parker off at his house and then drive around the neighborhood a couple of times. I don't want to go home, but I don't want to stay out.

After my third circuit, the fact that I'm wasting gas makes the decision for me. I head home and let out a breath when I get inside. Some of my tension leaks out with it, but most of it stays. I head upstairs and down the hall, past Amber's closed bedroom door. Small, high-pitched noises come from inside. Is she crying? This day sucks. Everyone's falling apart. I raise my hand to knock.

"Yeah, oh yeah. That feels good, baby."

Goddammit! I barge into her room—so glad her door doesn't lock—and freeze.

My sister is lying on her bed, naked, with a webcam trained on her. She shrieks and pulls a blanket over her. "Gotta go, babe. I'll chat ya later." She closes a window on the computer and then turns her famous glare on me. Its usual power is somewhat diminished by the fact that she's clutching a blanket and trying to hide. "What the hell is your problem?"

"My problem?" Why does this argument always start the same way? "I thought you had a guy in here."

"Well, I don't."

I gesture to the empty stretch of bed beside her and cross to the laptop. "No, you've just got one online." I yank the webcam free.

"Don't!" Amber half lunges before the blanket falls aside. She shrieks again and scrambles to cover up.

"I helped change your diapers," I say. "I've seen it all."

Her jaw falls open, and the horror on her face is almost comical. Almost. "That's not the point. Why can't you just stay out of my life?"

I hold up the webcam and back toward the door. "Because I can't, especially if I think you're getting taken advantage of."

"It's not taking advantage if I want it." Her brown eyes are practically on fire.

The thread holding my patience snaps. I pause in the doorway, webcam in a white-knuckled death grip. "Except you're fifteen!" I slam the door and storm down the hall to my bedroom. Inside, I throw the cam in the trash and then punch the wall. The pain grounds me a little. Molly, Amber, Ward—is anyone in my life not going to cause me grief today? I need to murder something.

I boot up a first-person-shooter, even though they are my least favorite type of game, and arm myself to the teeth. Time fades into the background as I shoot things, first on foot, then from a car going way above any recommended speed limit. It's amazingly therapeutic. There's me and the enemy. There are no feelings. There's no nonsense. It's fire and fire some more, and the enemy is toast.

Sometime later, my phone buzzes for a text. I finish clearing an area—this is not a time to leave anything alive—before snatching it off my nightstand.

New message from Molly.

I hit pause. Her name works like some kind of calming/raging drug on my body. I'm split again, this time into ignore-her-and-go-back-to-shooting-things and see-what-she-has-to-say-because-I-really-do-want-to-know-and-make-sure-she's-all-right. After a long moment where I alternate between looking at my phone and the controller, camp two wins. I breathe in and out, slow, and open the text.

Can we talk?

Chapter 18: Molly

an we talk?

C I hit send before I lose my nerve and toss my phone on the passenger seat. I'd raced back into A's only to have Nikki and Carla—my boss—tell me to go home and feel better. I tried to argue, but they weren't having it. Five minutes later, I gave in and left, which is turning out to be terrible therapy and bad for my vision. The sun is in my eyes, but I can't start the car yet. If I do, I'll drive home and not leave again, and that won't fix things with Craig

Craig, who I treated like crap. God, I'm a horrible idiot. I listened to Ward. Ward has never had my best interests in mind. Ward has always played games with me. Craig hasn't played one game other than M and M in the almost two weeks I've known him. Not that two weeks is a long time, but he's genuine. There's just something real about him that Ward doesn't have. There's a chance for us. At least, there might have been. I probably ruined it, and I can't even woman up and call him. I sent a text that he most likely won't even answer.

My phone buzzes.

I snatch it like some lovesick teenager who hasn't heard from her crush in five minutes. Get a grip. It might not even be him.

But it is.

Sure. Where?

The vice around my heart loosens. I draw my first deep breath in the last day. He isn't avoiding or ignoring me. He's not mad at me. Well, he's feeling charitable enough to respond. That's not quite the same thing.

Either way, I need an answer. A's is out, and I don't really want to have this talk in a coffee shop. After a minute, I decide on my house. My folks are at my aunt's for the day. My house will be quiet and private. That's what this conversation needs. I text him and wait. An *ok* comes a minute later, so I start Dessy and drive, my heart doing acrobatics the whole way. If the texts are any indication, this discussion is going to go horribly. He's not being talkative. Then again, it's tough to be talkative via text message.

Really, knock it off. You'll see him soon. By the end of the day, everything will be worked out, for better or worse.

I get to my house before him—phew. I don't know what I would have done if he beat me here, but this gives me a few minutes to relax. I get out of the car and beep her locked just as Craig's car stops at the curb. So much for collecting myself.

He gets out and walks up the driveway. His face is expressionless. At least he's not scowling.

"Hi," I say when he stops beside me.

"Hi." His voice is as blank as his face. Is this what he's like when he's angry? This is a quiet anger, the scary type.

All right, don't put emotions into the boy's heart. You did that a half hour ago, and remember how well that turned out? "Come on in."

I lead him to the door and inside. The living room isn't spotless, but it's not a mess either. I straighten the rug under the coffee table with my foot and then perch on the couch. Craig sits in the armchair across from me and relaxes into the plush leather. Relaxing is good, right?

"Can I get you a drink?" Nice, I sound like a waitress.

A spark of humor lights his green eyes, but it doesn't last. "I'm fine."

The silence starts and drags. Finally, I clear my throat. It's up to me, as it should be. I started this mess. "I owe you an apology for earlier."

No response.

Oh boy, this isn't good. There's nowhere but forward, though. I take a deep breath and plunge into the dark, uncertain waters ahead. "I was upset. I jumped to conclusions. I didn't hear you out." I stare at the floor. "And I'm sorry."

The silence lasts another eternity. I try to meet his gaze. When I can't manage that, I attempt to look anywhere but the floor. That fails about as epically, and I resign myself to waiting.

"Apology accepted," he says. "But what's going on?"

I exhale, and all the strength goes out of my muscles. Waiting for his confirmation took more than it should have. And the explanation is going to take even more. "I'll get to that in a second, but first, how do you know Ward?"

His eyebrows shoot up. "You know him?"

My confidence takes a swan dive underground. Ward didn't tell him about me. Ward never even mentioned me. I freaked out for nothing. I don't even deserve forgiveness. "He's my ex-boyfriend from college. We dated for almost two years when he ended it by letting me see him making out with another girl."

Craig stiffens, and his hands curl into fists.

I take a deep breath. "So when I saw you talking to him at Bob's like you were old friends, well, I assumed. Then when he cornered me by the bathrooms at A's—"

"He cornered you?" Craig's voice is almost a snarl.

I nod, unable to speak for a second. "Yeah. It was one of his typical make-Molly-feel-like-dragon-excrement visits. He said or implied that he told you all kinds of stuff about how disloyal and emotionally damaged I am. Then he basically said you were cheating on me, so I may as well quit now. I'm not sure why I listened. We aren't even officially anything, but when he started talking, all my insecurities came flooding back."

Craig is silent for a long time. Finally, he grunts. "Ward and I played at tournies in high school. I never really liked him, and I like him even less now."

My breath catches. Does he mean now as in the last day or as in the last five minutes because of my past?

"I left Bob's about twenty minutes after you did. I didn't text you because I thought you wanted to be left alone." He runs one hand over his face. "I wish you'd told me this yesterday."

I can't argue with that. "Me too. I just didn't know how." I sag back into the cushions. "Kind of like I don't know how to get rid of the hold Ward has on my self-esteem. I thought I had it under control, but yesterday and today proved me wrong. I'm still fighting the battle."

Craig leans forward and then jerks to a stop. Was he going to move closer? Did I say something to make him decide not to? His expression is blank for a moment, and then his face lights up. "Do you know how to play Chanter's?"

I flinch, but even so, a tiny piece of me is insulted. Of course I know how to play. "Yeah, why?"

136

"Do you have a deck?"

"Yeah." What does this have to do with anything? "Why?"

"Ward is at Bob's right now playing. You say you're fighting a battle. It's time you won."

My heart threatens to stop. I did not take that the way he meant it to be taken. "You mean …."

He holds out a hand. "I'll drive. I'll stay by your side the whole time. You can defeat him. I know you can because you're better than him."

I'm frozen. Craig's hand is more than an offer to come with me. It's a silent promise. It's the point of no return. If I go to Bob's, if I do this, I'm putting Ward behind me. I'm moving on. I'll be free, what I've wanted for so long.

Then why am I shaking? What's stopping me? I'm afraid of Ward, not Craig. Or am I afraid of being with Craig? I've been using my bad experiences, Ward in particular, as an excuse to hide and stay single. Craig is different, though. There's real caring and trust in his eyes, and it's all for me. I'd be a fool not to give this a try. And who am I kidding, I've wanted to since *Star Trek*.

I take his hand. "I'll get my deck."

Five minutes later, we're in his car on our way to Bob's, and I have the deck in a white-knuckled death grip. There's a big difference between sitting in my living room and thinking and actually going to the store and confronting my past. My body's shaking the worst it ever has.

Craig pats my shoulder when he stops at a red light. "Relax."

"I'm trying." Except it's not working. I'm drumming my fingernails on the armrest at about a million clicks a second, and every breath is the fast, shallow kind.

"Try harder," he says, taking a left. He already knows me too well.

I stop tapping the armrest and force myself to take slower inhalations. I don't have to be calm. I just have to appear calm. I am Iron Man, strong as steel and indestructible.

Craig pulls into Bob's lot and gets a spot two rows back. Somehow, I force myself out of the car and toward the store. Clouds have rolled in, covering the early evening sky in grayish white. That's fine. This isn't a sunny moment.

Craig opens the door and holds it.

I stumble past him. "I might hate you for this." My voice shakes a little.

"That's fine," he says, following me inside. "You can change your feelings later. Right now, do whatever it takes. You've got this, and I'll be here through the hate and all."

The aisles and games and figurines pass in a blur, and the next thing I know, we're at the door to the back room. Craig knocks, and I lean against the wall.

Ward's muffled *come in* comes from inside. Somehow, it makes Dawn's ominous *enter* seem not scary in the slightest.

"Ready?" Craig says.

I take a deep breath and let it out, slow. It's now or never, literally. If I don't do this, I'll never come back, and it's time. "I was born ready."

Craig smiles a little and opens the door.

Ward looks up from his game. He has a bunch of creatures, and his opponent has nothing but power cards. "Craig." His gaze lands on me, and he licks his lips. "And Molly. So you didn't listen to me, and I was just trying to help."

I can't speak. My vocal cords are frozen, and even if they weren't, what would I say? Craig gives me a little push forward and pats my lower back.

That's my cue. I force my mouth open. "You didn't tell me anything worth listening to." My voice is shaking even worse now. Words came out, though. That's a regular miracle.

"Really?" Ward rotates some of his creature cards to the left to attack. "Twenty damage to you. You are dead, my friend."

The guy glares and shoves his cards into their box.

"Who's next?" Ward says, gathering his cards and stacking them in his signature smug victory dance. "Craig, you in? Maybe you could make up for how bad I killed you yesterday."

Ward's words punch me in the stomach. He gave Craig a beating? Granted, it was only Chanter's, but right now, that doesn't matter. He's still hurting people. He's recently hurt someone I care about. That's not okay, and he's not dealing Craig more damage.

"No. He's not." I step forward, the tiniest bit of confidence entering my body. It's time. "But I am."

Ward's entire demeanor changes. Suddenly, he's a hunter, and I'm wounded prey.

"How unexpected." He gestures to the now-empty seat across from him. "Have a seat, Molls."

I do and extract my deck from its box. It's silver with a little bit of a few different mechanics. If memory and the brief glance I got of Ward's cards just now are correct, his preferred deck is black and red—deck-replenish and fire. If I can keep myself together, this should be an evenly matched game. I shuffle and draw eight cards—four power cards, two spells, and two creatures. If it wouldn't be a telltale, I'd smile. It's a better-than-decent starting hand.

Ward finishes shuffling, draws, and cuts to see who goes first. "Power cost two."

I cut a creature and conceal another smile. "Three." More

good luck.

Ward grunts and puts the top half of his deck back in place. "Go."

With pleasure. The burst of confidence is growing. I reorganize my hand, cheapest to most expensive play cost, and play a power.

Ward clucks his tongue. "Silver still? And here I thought you might have made a better deck." He plays a red-black power with some special ability and sits back in his chair. "Your turn." His face, his posture—everything about him means intimidation. It worked on me for years.

It won't work now. I draw and get a creature card that needs four powers to play. That claws a little at my confidence shield. I put the card into my hand and play another power.

The aura of predator around Ward increases. He plays a red power and engages that and the one he played before to hit me with a spell. "Four damage to player."

Crap. My hand moves in slow motion to my life counter and freezes upon contact. Like that, I'm down to sixteen. I doubt this is the exact deck he played with six months ago, but it's still built to kill and kill fast. That's red's specialty, and silver is the worst color to combat that. Much like our relationship, he's ahead from the start, and I'm left to fumble behind and clean up the mess he makes of me.

No, focus. I can beat him. I can. I just need to stay alive a few more turns. The question is, can I?

I draw another card—a spell that allows me to redirect another spell—and play a power. Ward tilts his head in a show of fake concern and plays a one-damage insta-attack creature. That's another point off my life, and I take my turn, playing my fourth power. I now have enough for my creature, but something stops me. Silver isn't about strength. It's about cunning. If I engage all my power cards, I'll be left defenseless, an all-too-familiar feeling.

"Your turn."

Ward draws, engages three, and plays a spell. "Five damage to player."

Double crap. I reach for my life counter but stop. He played a spell. I can do something. I engage my power and play my own spell. "Redirect. Five damage to you."

His eyes go wide, and anger sparks in their depths. He blinks, and his smarm is back. "Not bad. Five whole points that you didn't even give with your own cards." He turns his life counter to fifteen. "Your turn."

Fifteen. Fifteen, we're even, and who cares if I didn't deal the damage myself. As he's said so many times, it's not how you deal it, only that it's dealt. He's lost as many points as I have, and like that, I know how I'm going to win this game. My fifth power goes down, and I sit back to wait. I'm not his victim anymore.

"Got nothing, huh?" He draws and plays another damage spell, which I reflect back at him.

So it goes. A few turns later, he has a few more insta-attack creatures. I play my own creature to block some of that damage, all the while sending his damage spells back at him. My life goes down, but not as fast as his does. My growing power reserves let me turn his game against him. He falls, fast, and there's no recovering for him.

But there is for me. My heartbeat gets stronger with every point of damage he takes. I've been so afraid of him, so afraid of how he made me feel. I've been an idiot and weak. He's nothing, a nobody to me, and I'm done letting him have power.

141

"Eight damage," I say after stealing one of his creatures and attacking. "Game."

Behind me, Craig gives a hum of approval. The sound goes right to my blood, warming me from the inside out.

Ward, by contrast, snarls and slams his counter to twenty with a vengeance. "Rematch."

I tuck my cards back into the box. "No. I've given you your rematch. It's not my fault if you can't handle losing to me."

Ward is out of his seat and lunging across the table, hand out and fingers splayed.

Craig smacks him away. "Don't touch her."

"Shut up, pretty boy." Ward turns his anger on me. "He won't stay. You'll be wishing you didn't break up with me."

As if a storm ends, sun breaks through the clouds in my mind. Ward is pissed. That's all it is. His ego can't handle that I left him. I've been walking around like a zombie over a three year old who lost a shiny toy.

Well, that's over, now. I make sure the box is closed, stand, and take Craig's hand. "No, I don't think I will." I lead Craig out of the room.

"Ask him about the girl I saw him with last night," Ward says as the door closes. He shouts something else, but it's muffled.

It doesn't matter. I'm done with Ward. I march back through the store as if I'm wearing blinders. The door is my goal. Nothing is getting between me and it, nothing.

Outside, I face Craig and let out a breath. "How did I do?"

His grin is as bright as my new sun. "You were magical." And he kisses me.

Chapter 19: Craig

She's amazing, and kissing her is amazing.

I pull back and wrap an arm around her shoulders. "You were brilliant, and I'm buying you dinner. Where do you want to go?"

She sags against me, which feels a little too good. "If it's all the same to you, I don't think I'm up for a restaurant. Unless you want to eat out, then we can eat out, but we don't have to—"

"Whoa." I put a finger to her lips. "You're rambling, and eating in is fine." My stomach flips. Well, as long as we don't eat at my place. I don't need a naked Amber wandering around. But how do I get that across without mentioning my sister issues?

"Do you want pizza? I have frozen pizza at my house." Or maybe she'll handle it. "Wow, I'm a pathetic host."

"You are not pathetic." I squeeze her shoulders. If anyone's terrible here, it's me. She just stood up to her abusive ex, and all I can think about is my own problems. The important part of this evening is Molly. Dragon droppings would be fine for dinner as long as I'm eating with her. "Pizza sounds great."

We pile into my car, and I drive to her house. She lets us in, and we kick our shoes off. Again, the artwork in the living room hits me. It's got heart in a way I haven't seen before. It also goes well with the dark furniture and green walls.

"Nice pictures," I say.

She blushes. "Thanks. I worked hard on them."

That stops me dead. "You did those? Like, on the computer?" Oh man, I sound like a tool. And duh, on the computer. She's a graphic designer.

"Yeah." She stops beside a picture of a couple on a moonlit beach. "They were my thesis project for undergrad."

"Wow." I examine an image of two dogs running through a field with woods in the background. "I hope you've given serious consideration to where you're going with your career. You've got a gift."

She goes quiet and still. There's a chance she's hiding something, but if she wants to keep an inconsequential secret about her uncertain professional future, that's fine. She deserves it after rocking so much earlier. "I've thought about it a bit." She shakes her head and comes back to the present. "But I'll figure it out later. I'm hungry." She paces into the kitchen, which is painted some shade of yellow that I can't name, and turns the temperature dial on the oven to four fifty. "So that's going to take a bit. Do you want a drink or a snack or something?"

"Water?" I say, studying the stuff on the counter. There's the usual—sugar, coffee, bread—and then there's a familiar box. I close the distance and pick up the Spock cereal. "You bought this too?"

Molly pauses from getting two glasses out of a cabinet. "Oh, yeah. I saw it, and it kind of followed me home." She fills the glasses from the tap and holds one out to me.

I take the glass and shake the cereal a little. "I was in the process of getting one of these when Nikki cornered me to ask about the movie."

Molly laughs. "That sounds like her. Though, it looks like we may have been meant to go to that movie together."

"Indeed," I say, and my phone buzzes. No, not now. I'm not dealing with Amber tonight, or worse, I'm not even acknowledging Ward. I shouldn't even check it, but my responsible side won't let me ignore it.

Thankfully, it's none of those. It's Lyd, and there's, blessedly, no mention of my sister. She's just asking about the next M and M session. I shoot her a quick response that it's not tonight and put my phone away. I'm done with the cheap piece of plastic for the evening.

"Something wrong?" Molly's voice is soft, and there's a ton of uncertainty in her eyes.

I gulp some of my water. "No. Just Lyd." I freeze. Ward shouted about Lyd as we were leaving, and now I mention her. Smooth, Craig. "It was just friend time last night."

She blinks. "What?"

Goddammit, I'm going to kill Ward if I ever see him again. Things just got onto solid ground here. I'm not letting this deteriorate. "As we were leaving, Ward yelled for you to ask me about Lydia. I went out with her last night, but it was just friend time."

Her eyes go glassy for a second. "I didn't hear anything about Lydia. He said to ask about the girl, but I didn't think he named her. I assumed it was just another pathetic attempt on his part."

Open mouth. Insert foot. Nice work, you moron. Though, I've started. May as well finish. "Well, he did, and I want to lay it all out now. There's nothing, and never has been, anything

145

between Lyd and me. We've been best friends since before we could talk."

"That's awesome." Her voice is honest and lacks any kind of fear or jealousy. "Must be great to have someone like a sister."

Every muscle in my body tenses. "It's great to have Lyd." So much for not thinking about Amber. "My actual sister is a lot less awesome."

"Younger or older?"

Younger, way too much younger. "She's fifteen."

Molly pats my arm. "I'm so sorry."

That drags a smile out of me. "Thanks."

The oven beeps, perfectly cutting off that conversation. Molly puts the pizza in and sets the microwave timer. "T-ten minutes."

"And counting," I say and then do an imitation of the Count from *Sesame Street*'s laugh. "Do you have cutting implements and a board?"

"Actually, I was thinking we'd just play tug of war and then fold whatever portion we end up with into sandwiches." Her voice and face are completely serious.

I blink. There's a moment of silence, and then we both start laughing.

"That was good," I say when I stop.

"Thanks." She turns and pulls a wooden cutting board from a cabinet beneath the sink. Then she opens a drawer and extracts a pizza cutter … with a freakin' finger guard.

"Are you serious?" I take the cutter, twist it around to examine it from all angles, and then hold it up in a sword salute parody. "Oh mighty pizza cutter plus two of cheesiness."

Molly licks her lips. "I usually refer to it as plus five."

I'm speechless. From someone who's seemed afraid of geek,

that's a huge turnaround. It's official. Girl's got my heart.

I toss the pizza cutter of plus whatever on the counter, gather her in my arms, and kiss her, long and slow. There's something in this moment, something calm and gentle. I pull her close, and she wraps her arms around my neck. Before I know I've moved, I have her against the fridge, and we're lost in each other. I can't get enough. Her cherry scent surrounds me, and I start to lose it. She feels so good against me like this.

The timer goes off, the beeps tearing the moment to shreds.

Somehow, I pull away. My breaths come fast, and only the knowledge that the quiet dinner she wanted will be ruined keeps me from ignoring the microwave.

"What was that for?" she asks, a little breathless herself. Her cheeks are flushed, and her lips are a deep pink, beckoning me.

It takes everything I have not to give into the siren. Instead, I kiss her nose. "For being awesome."

I let her out from between me and the fridge, and she gets the pizza. A few end pieces of cheese are a little charred, but it's totally worth it.

"Can I cut it?" I say, picking up the cutter.

She puts the pizza on the counter. "You just wanna use that thing."

Actually, I just wanna continue where we left off, only on the couch, but the cutter does hold a level of interest. "Guilty."

She steps aside. "All yours."

I take her place and make a few deft strokes with the cutter—one down and two small diagonals. "Voila."

She stares at the pizza, then at me and then back at the pizza. "Did you just cut a peace sign pattern?"

Victory. I officially want this girl. She doesn't think my peace sign pizza is stupid. "Yes, yes I did. Observe the mighty powers of the plus five pizza slicing implement." I do the sword salute parody again, and bits of cheese fly around the kitchen. Oops.

Molly laughs and plucks the cutter from my hand. "Smooth." She tosses the plus fiver in the sink and swipes a larger slice of pizza. "I feel like I should offer you beer to go with the pizza, but I don't think I have any."

"It's fine," I say between mouthfuls. This is no time to do my impression of Parker eating gummy bears. "I'm happy." The truth of those last words washes over me like a stream touched by sunlight. It's warm and embracing and true. I've never been this happy with a girl before, never, and more than anything, I want this to last.

A door opens somewhere.

"Hello?" an unfamiliar female voice says.

Molly freezes for a second and then sets down her pizza slice. "Hi, Mom."

Oh crap, I wasn't planning on meeting the parents this soon. No time like the present, it seems.

An older version of Molly, only with blonde hair, strolls into the kitchen, a taller, dark-haired man behind her. She smiles at her daughter and then gives me a curious look.

"Mom, Dad, this is Craig." Molly gestures to me.

I hold out my hand. "It's very nice to meet you …." Uh-oh, I don't know Molly's last name.

Lucky for me, her mom is apparently easy to win over. She takes my hand as if a handshake is some ritual of kindness. "Karen," she says. Must be her name. "It's very nice to meet you too." She releases my hand. Dad moves in for the kill, and I concentrate on appearing relaxed. This is no big deal. I'm a nice guy. Her dad's bound to like me. He shakes my hand without trying to break my wrist in the traditional man-shake manner. He even gives me an approving nod.

"How did it go?" Molly says when the parental introductions are done.

"Fine," her dad says. There's a CEO type of authority in his voice. "She's moved into the new apartment, and her house is clean." He yawns. "And I'm ready to sleep for three years."

"Only three?" her mom says, biting off her own yawn. "Any news?"

Molly goes stiff. That's quite the reaction to a two-word question. "No."

Her mom finishes the yawn she couldn't quite stop. "No news is good news." She points to the ceiling. "At any rate, as your father said, we're exhausted. So we'll see you in the morning. Craig, lovely to meet you, and you two have fun."

Her folks do the awkward offspring-is-in-the-house-with-significant-other wave and wander out of the kitchen. Their footsteps echo on stairs and then on the second floor before a door closes.

"They like you," Molly says when it's quiet again.

I polish off another bite of pizza. "That was fast."

She shrugs. "Considering my past relationships."

Hint taken. That's enough of that topic. Ward's been enough of an issue today. Issue, which reminds me. "I don't want to get too far into your business, so tell me if I am. But the news your mom asked about. Is everything okay?"

The stiffness returns to Molly's posture. She takes a bite of pizza and chews extra slowly. "I'm okay, yes." There's definitely more to that. "It's not me specifically. She was asking about the piles of job applications I sent out in the last month. We need cash, bad. Dad was on the corporate rise. Then his company downsized, and you can guess where it went from there."

I can, and it's not pretty. "I'm sorry."

"Not your fault," she says. "It is what it is, but he hasn't been able to find substantial work since. Funds are tight. Mom's income doesn't cover it, and I'm almost desperate to find something." She takes her last bite of pizza and brushes her hands off. "Like Mom said, though, no news is good news."

I nod. What other response is there? The news thing is right. Silence isn't a rejection, but it isn't an acceptance either. I'm living the broke college student life now, but I know I have my summer job starting soon. Without that … it's unthinkable, but what comfort can I offer?

"So," Molly says after a short silence. Or maybe she'll save me by changing the subject. "Not sure if you're interested, but my folks have all the original *Star Trek* episodes on DVD."

A light bulb goes on in my head. Cuddle time—the perfect comfort. Words will be hollow at this point, but closeness will say everything I feel. Besides, it's *Star Trek.* How can I say no? "No wonder you know them."

She blushes. She's been doing that a lot, not that I'm complaining. Pink is a good color for her. "I grew up watching them, but if you don't want to—"

"Don't be ridiculous. Of course I wanna watch *Star Trek* with you."

She doesn't blush this time, but she does go still and just watch me for a minute. It's as if she can't believe that I said yes. "Follow." She leads me back into the living room, but something's different. There's purpose in her movements. It's confidence. That's what's been missing pretty much since the first time I saw her. The confidence she showed that first night at A's has been gone. It's back now, though, and the change is beautiful. Even with the financial troubles, confronting Ward made a difference. I actually helped her.

She plugs a disc into the player, and I flop on the couch. The opening credits come on—that song rocks—and Molly darts back into the kitchen.

"Love that song," she says, sitting next to me and handing me one of the smaller slices of pizza.

We settle into the leather and lapse into silence. This is so right and so comfortable. I could just sit next to her all night.

"Oh," Molly says after a bit.

I jump. "What? What's wrong?"

She shakes her head and points to the screen. It's the tranya scene. The line about relishing the drink passes, delivered with the precision only *Star Trek* can pull off.

"It's official now," I say. "I was meant to order that drink."

"And I may have been meant to serve it to you." She finishes her pizza and scoots closer until she's right against me.

A thrill shoots through my blood. She fits like she was made to be there. Her slow, even breaths tickle the exposed skin of my arm, and I tingle all over. My thoughts go to Ludacris speed, and I force them to slow. This isn't about the physical. This is about feeling, and she deserves to feel cared for, wanted.

Maybe even loved.

I wrap an arm around her shoulders, and she rests her head on my chest. This is right. This is perfect.

"Thank you," she says so soft I almost miss it.

"You're welcome." I run my hand over her hair and rest my cheek on top of her head. There is no better way to spend a Saturday night.

Chapter 20: Molly

I slide my piece closer to Craig's and sit back in my chair. The last four days have been something out of the best romantic comedy ever not made. Between M and M and general nutty fun with Craig, I can't get enough of life.

"'Have we not lost it yet?'" Sonya says, panting and in character.

"You have," Dawn says. "But you are now lost."

"Wonderful," I say. This is not how this session was supposed to go. By the worst turn of fate, we've maneuvered our characters into a labyrinth complete with magical danger and random tasks to complete. So far we've almost lost Sonya to a pit and had to run, screaming—well, Parker screamed, loudly—from a band of mutated ogres. Now I know why Craig gets a horrified expression every time Dawn says anything remotely surprising or threatening. At this rate, it will be a miracle if we get out of here in two pieces, each.

"You come to a fork in the path," Dawn says.

Craig twitches.

Dawn continues, undeterred. "The left path is pitch dark, and there is a slight glow coming from the right."

"Left," Sonya says without even a nanosecond of hesitation.

"Strange glowing hallways are never good."

"Neither are pitch dark hallways," Lydia says from Craig's other side. She came in five minutes late, sat down, and has barely spoken. Craig's one attempt at conversation was met with a scowl and silence. He's been super quiet ever since and keeps darting glances at her when she's not looking.

Sonya shrugs. "But glowing pathways are usually worse."

"Enough bickering." Parker waves his arms in the air. The guy is nuts, but he's kind of fun. "Piff the Eviscerator will use his great arcana knowledge to decide our fates." He grabs his D20 and does some weird shimmy dance. He lets it fall, and his face follows suit. "Three plus nine is twelve."

"There is a glowing hallway," Dawn says. "It is probably caused by magic."

Lydia snorts. "My plus zero would have told me that."

"Silence, Elf," Parker says. Sometimes it's impossible to tell if it's him or Piff speaking. "Unless you believe you can do better."

In response, Lydia holds up her character sheet and taps it, presumably where the plus zero is located. "Zero, as in nothing."

"Same here," Sonya says.

"I have a plus one," Craig says.

Lydia tosses down her sheet and folds her arms. "Well, there we go. We're screwed."

"Not necessarily." Craig turns to me. "What do you have?"

I check my sheet. "A plus one."

"Like I said," Lydia says under her breath. "We're screwed."

"Oh stop being so pessimistic." Sonya sits up straight and taps her character sheet. "Arcana isn't the only skill we have. You're a ranger. Stealth down there and see if you see anything."

Lydia brightens a fraction. "Worth a shot. Can I use stealth here?"

Dawn shuffles her papers. "You may use whatever you think may be of assistance."

"Stealth it is, then." Lydia rolls without fanfare. The die lands, and she slams her fist on the table. "Total of thirteen, lovely. It's not even worth it."

"I'll give it a shot. I'm trained in stealth too." I roll a sixteen and can't help a grin. "Total of twenty-five."

"Nice." Craig claps my shoulder.

"Thanks." I lean forward to move my token and catch sight of Lydia. She's glaring at me as if I just stole her favorite stuffed animal. Is a stealth roll that important to her?

"Very good," Dawn says. "You sneak down the lit hallway, remaining quiet and relatively hidden. You see nothing of any danger that you can identify and return to your companions."

"Well, if there's nothing, we may as well go for it," Sonya says.

Parker gives an exaggerated nod. "Piff the Eviscerator agrees."

"Shifter, Elf?" Dawn says.

"I'm down," Craig says.

Lydia stares at the board for a minute. Finally, she shrugs and flips her hand. "Fine by me." Her voice is flat.

"All right, this is getting ridiculous." Sonya plants her hands on the table and leans toward Lydia. "What the hell is the matter with you? You've been a dark cloud since you got here, and you're dragging everyone down."

Lydia bares her teeth. "Am I? Gee, I'm so sorry. I didn't realize I wasn't allowed to have a bad day." She stands and storms out.

The room falls silent. I pretend to study my character sheet.

I don't want my gaze to give away all my questions. Is she always like this? I mean, obviously she's not if Sonya's calling her out, but is she like this often? Is she even going to come back? Do any of them know why she's upset?

"Don't," Sonya says, breaking through my thoughts.

Craig is poised halfway to standing. He looks to the table, then to the door, then to Sonya and back to the door. "This isn't like her."

"I know." Sonya holds up a finger. "But clearly she needs a minute for whatever reason. Let her go."

Craig holds his position for another few minutes. That can't be comfortable, but he doesn't seem to be straining. He casts one more concerned glance to the door and then sits, pulling his chair back up to the table. "Let's check out this lit room." His voice lacks some of its usual enthusiasm.

"You make your way down the hall and into the lighted space," Dawn says as if nothing's happened. Maybe nothing has. "A single crystal affixed to one wall provides the light. Before you is a door with no handle—"

"Then how do we know it is a door?" Parker says, possibly as Piff.

Dawn gives him her one-eyed glare. "Because your gracious GM just told you, but if you feel the need to have someone in your group check with perception, be my guest."

"I've got it," Craig says, picking up his D20. "I have an eighteen wis." He rolls and thunks his head against his hand. "One, right, so ten."

Dawn gives Parker an I-told-you-so stare, except however that would come out in Dawn speak. "Luckily for you, a ten is enough to know that the rectangular slab of metal is, in fact, a door. There is a small pad, the height and width of a human

155

hand, on the wall beside it. Course of action?"

"Sounds like a case for an arcana check." Lydia retakes her seat, setting down a glass of water. She presses her fingers to her temples and winces.

Craig sits up straighter. "Headache? Why didn't you say so?"

"It's fine," she says, a little sharply. "Really. I just took some meds." She lowers her hands. "I'll be fine. Sorry about that, guys."

Craig pats her shoulder. Sonya and Parker give her reassuring glances. Dawn doesn't move, but her eyes soften. I make a note to ask Craig about this later and offer a smile. Headaches shouldn't cause that level of anger.

"As we were saying," Dawn says, back in GM mode. "There is a door with no handle and a matching plate."

Parker picks up his D20. "This is a job for Piff the Mighty Eviscerator."

He does his funky rolling dance again, and Sonya mutters something about additional nicknames. Parker rolls a twenty-one total, and we all sit forward. Finally, we'll get actual information.

"You know the pad activates some kind of latent magic when touched," Dawn says.

Parker moves his hand in circles above the board and mutters. Is this him casting a spell? "I touch the pad."

"Something clicks in the floor." Dawn flips pages in her binder. "Three panels appear on the door, each showing a picture. The first is of a woman, the second of a man, and the third a shadowy form."

Sonya groans. "A riddle. Why are there always riddles in these types of caves?"

"Because caves wouldn't be complete without riddles," Lydia

says. Her voice is a bit stronger and much less frustrated. "A man, a woman, and a figure. Any thoughts? My first thought is some kind of anthropomorph."

"Incorrect," Dawn says.

Lydia gives a palms-up. "Or not. Anyone else?"

"Well," Sonya says, tapping her chin. "Man and woman could mean romance. So maybe the third is a child?"

"Closer," Dawn says.

"Do you want specifics?" I say. "Daughter or son?"

"No."

"No, what?" Sonya says. "No to daughter? No to son? Or no to child in general?"

Craig rubs his forehead. "I'm confused."

"That makes two of us," I say. I'm with Sonya here. Riddles suck.

"Enough." Parker punches the air. "I grow tired of guessing. Piff the Eviscerator flies up to the door. 'Hermiog Thermiog, methledion, Eptius filmeptius miggery flig!'"

Dawn covers her mouth with her hand. "Nothing happens." Her voice shakes with the beginnings of laughter.

We all stare at Parker, and then we all exchange a look. It's not a child. It's not an anthropomorph. It's not a bunch of random words randomly thrown together in response to a random riddle.

Lydia's the first to break the circle of silent questions. "Please tell me we don't need to speak the Elvish word for *friend*."

"You do not." Dawn lowers her hand. "I will give you a hint, though. By the riddle's text, child could be the answer, but it is not."

Sonya snaps her fingers. "Love."

Parker frowns. "In Elvish?"

"Correct, Dwarf. The door clicks and swings open."

Sonya leans back in her chair. "Oh, that was easy. Pardon me while I vanish in a puff of logic."

"Yeah," Lydia says, her voice quiet. "Easy. Can we take a break?"

Craig rests his hand on her shoulder. "Do you need to call it quits?"

She pulls away. "No." She stands but doesn't move for a long moment. Finally, she sags. "Actually, yeah. I'm in a lot of pain. I'll see you guys later."

There's a chorus of goodbyes, mine included. Sonya calls a break and says she'll walk Lydia out. Lydia tries to shrug her off, but Sonya grabs her arm and marches her to the door. Dawn holds up a hand, and they pause in the doorway, so she can tell Lydia she won't lose xp for missing the session.

"Thanks for your help." Sonya wanders into the hall. "If you hadn't asked about Elvish, we wouldn't have gotten a clue, and I wouldn't have figured out love. Go team."

Lydia freezes in the doorway. Her gaze goes to Craig so fast it might be unconscious. She blinks and glances away with a vengeance. "Yeah, no problem."

She takes her leave, and the sudden absence hits me in the chest. Love, the way she just looked at Craig—she loves him or, at least, likes him a lot. Something slimy wriggles through my gut. Then I show up, and her hopes die. Not that they had a foundation. Craig said he doesn't like her like that, and as Nikki put it that first night at A's, they have the friends-since-the-womb aura. Still, that can't make it any easier for her.

And I can't say anything. It's not my place. I don't want to embarrass Lydia. She doesn't seem like a bad person at all. Unrequited love and the feel of being second, though, I can relate to. It's not a reason to hate her, and I don't want her to hate me, especially if we're going to be playing M and M together. If I say anything to Craig, though, she will, and he'll feel terrible. I clamp down on my new desire to have everything out in the open. This is up to them.

A few minutes later, Sonya strolls back into the room, phone in hand. She finishes sending a text and tosses her phone on the table. "So I, and thus by extension, we, have been invited to a party next Saturday."

"What kind of party?" Craig says. He's getting back to his normal self. Apparently it's true what they say about guys being clueless.

"Costume." Sonya sits. "Geek-ish themed. It's a graduation party for someone I know, and she just wants as many people as possible. Her words, not mine."

"Sounds intriguing," Dawn says. "Unfortunately, I have work, so I will not be attending."

"It's all good." Sonya fixes the rest of us with a glare. "But you're all coming."

"That does not sound like a question," Parker says.

Sonya pats his head. "It's not. I really don't want to go alone."

"Well, we cannot leave the maiden to travel alone. I will attend." Parker snaps and holds up a finger, eureka-style. "And I have the perfect costume."

Sonya closes her eyes as if in pain. "It better not be a gummy bear. Craig, Molly?"

"I'm up for it," Craig says, turning to me. "If you are."

Warmth gathers in my chest. He's leaving it up to me. There's a silent question in his eyes. Am I comfortable with such a public display of geekdom?

159

Well, am I? I take an inventory of my body. No sweaty palms. No shakes. No stomach clenching or muscles clenching or contracting heart, quickened breathing, twitching, finger-tapping urges, upset stomach … right, enough sounding like a list of drug side effects. I'm nerve-free, and dare I say it, the idea of a geeky costume party is … exciting.

"Sounds like fun."

"Awesome." Sonya picks up her phone. "I'll tell her I'm bringing a group."

I hear her words, but they don't register. Nothing registers but the sparkle in Craig's green eyes.

"It will be fun." He takes my hand. "Promise."

I squeeze his hand. Of course it will.

Chapter 21: Craig

I push open the door to Chloe's. Fluorescent lights run along the ceiling, illuminating aisles of crafts, games, figures, and tons of other things I don't have names for. The place is the love child of a jewelry store and a hobby shop on some very strong illegal substance.

It's also my last resort. The last three days have been dedicated to finding an appropriately geeky, girly gift for Molly. She agreed to go to a costume party for dorks. This is huge and requires a gift. That is, it requires a gift if I can find one. Bob's doesn't sell that kind of stuff, and jewelry store employees all looked at me like I had three heads—lion, goat, and dragon to be specific. If Chloe's doesn't have something, I'm in trouble.

I hook a right down an aisle of shiny objects. Charm bracelets and gaudy rings wink at me from both sides. It's like the attack of the shimmer creatures. I step closer to the bracelets until the onslaught lessens. My eyes and interests thank me. A bracelet is the way to go for Molly.

A few minutes into the search, though, I know it's a lost cause. They're all so generic—flowers, suns and moons, hearts. Gah. I leave the aisle and take up the search again. It's not that she wouldn't like one of those. She probably would. It's just not me and her. It's not what I want to give her.

"Can I help you?" A tall woman—or maybe a short woman in tall heels—steps in front of me. Her blonde hair is in a bun atop her head, and she glitters almost as much as the shimmer attack. How many items of jewelry is she wearing?

This is going to be a disaster. Cue the expert avoidance skills. I start to turn and give her the standard *no, just looking,* but one of her rings catches my eye. It's a castle or a crown. Either way, it's the right level of geeky for her to maybe be useful.

"Yeah." I face her. "I'm looking for a bracelet for my girlfriend." The word slides off my tongue, natural as anything. I haven't really asked Molly yet, and neither of us has made it official. Nevertheless, it feels perfect to say it. "But I'm looking for something … gamer-ish."

The woman's eyes light up. "Follow me."

I hesitate. It's probably the years of too many lame horror movies, but there's just something about those words coming from a seemingly harmless person. In the movies, this is where the unsuspecting idiot gets trapped in the portal of gelatinous, man-eating things from beyond. I follow before my pause becomes noticeable. There's something wrong with me.

Nice, normal store-worker woman leads me to an aisle toward the back of the store. The glitter monster has been here too, but I don't have to close my eyes and wait for the spots to disappear this time. This is fortunate because this aisle is exactly what I search for. I've died and gone to the land of geeky jewelry. There are dragon bracelets, medallion necklaces, and serpent ankle bracelets. Hell, there are even a few tiaras. How have I never seen this part of the store before?

"Is this what you're looking for?" the woman asks.

I blink out of the geek-heaven fog. "Yes." My voice comes

out slow as if I'm half asleep. "Thank you, fairy godmother."

She smiles the smile of the satisfied store worker. "All right, I'll be around if you need anything else." Her heels clack on the linoleum as she retreats.

"Thank you." But my speech is delayed again, and the pull of the fog has me. This aisle is worse than a pendulum in the hypnotism department. I need an anti-distraction spell, if such a thing exists. The party is only a couple of hours away, and I still need to get home, get changed and … and drive Amber to her friend's house.

That snaps me out of my reverie. Shop, pay, leave— preferably quickly so I don't have to listen to my sister complain about being late to her sleepover. And so the search begins anew. The castle/crown ring the saleswoman wore is here, but it doesn't match what I'm going for. I want something more … Molly and me. I riffle through some other rings. There's a pi one, but I toss it aside. It's too much like Bob's and everything Bob's symbolizes. Maybe not a ring, anyway. Rings suggest hardcore commitment, and I don't wanna scare her off. Back to the bracelet idea, and there are plenty to choose from. I start at one end and work my way across—dragons, serpents, Arthurian-themed, dice.

Dice?

Bingo. I unfasten the clasp and take down the bracelet, which is a silver chain connecting a D4, 6, 8, 10, 12, 20, and percentile. Perfect isn't accurate enough for this discovery. Loot in hand, I head back toward the front of the store, grabbing an appropriately dice-patterned gift box.

My helper is working checkout. She gives me a smile when I present the bracelet. "Good choice. I hope she likes it."

I pay before she gives me a price. "I know she will."

Ten minutes later, I'm home and can't find a parking space. My usual spot in the driveway is taken up by some ridiculously expensive car. Seriously, my four years of college cost less than this thing. Both sides of the street are mobbed too, forcing me to park around the corner and then jog back to my house to make up for the precious seconds I just lost. Why is my neighborhood a parking lot?

The second I step into my house, my confusion disappears. Right, Mom and Dad are having their annual Tupperware party, as if anyone has Tupperware parties anymore. How did I forget? It's the reason I'm Amber's transportation, an engagement for which I am officially late. I take the steps two at a time and dash down the hall.

"Where have you been?" Amber is camped out on the floor across from my bedroom, duffle in her lap. "I'm gonna be late."

I throw my bedroom door open. "You and me both." Door closed, I change into my Spock costume and tuck the box with the bracelet into my pocket. Because this is technically a date, I run a comb through my hair. It doesn't help much, but my stress levels are roughly at plugging-finger-into-a-power-socket levels. The bad hair is to be expected.

"Craig?" Amber's whine comes from the hall. "Come on."

I check my reflection one more time. I look like Spock, and I won't scare small children. That's good enough, and I open the door. "Let's go."

Amber's impatient scowl turns to a mask of horror. "Tell me you aren't parading past Mom's guests dressed like that."

"Can't." I pull the door closed and start down the hall. "Let's move."

Amber mumbles something about how it's not worth being seen with me to get to her friend's, and I bite my lip to keep from blurting that I'd have no problem with her staying home. It's bad enough that I'm going to have to speed to get to Molly's in time. My sister, of course, can't just be thankful that she has a ride at all. Could be worse, though. I could be wearing a red shirt.

Mom's waiting at the bottom of the stairs, standing as to block the view from the dining room where her guests are. It's almost as if she's embarrassed about what I'm wearing. Probably because she is. I pause outside her blocking sphere, and she shifts to accommodate. Maybe if she'd listened or cared about the webcam incident, I'd care more about embarrassing her. As it is, I can't muster the effort.

"I'm taking your daughter to her friend's house," I say.

Mom adjusts the top of her strapless dress. Where does she think she is, the Ritz? "Thank you, Craig." She steps forward for a hug that she uses to herd me toward the door.

What I wouldn't give for another of her *friends* to stroll inside right now.

"Have fun tonight, both of you. See you later." She kisses my cheek, and the unmistakable scent of rum colors her breath. Wonderful, she'll be shattered in no time.

Amber pulls away from her own cheek-kiss. "Thanks. See ya." She goes outside, not bothering to wait for the driver.

Mom walks away, and I let out a slow, controlled breath. Shouting isn't the answer. I follow Amber out. She's standing in the driveway, staring at the expensive car as if it's going to magically morph into mine.

"Had to park on the next street," I say as I pass her. "And this limo doesn't do curb pickup."

She falls into step beside me, dragging her feet. "You know you look like a dork, right?"

"That's the point." My voice comes out giddy, no shame. I'm away from the house. I'll be rid of my sister and have Molly soon. Let the party begin.

Amber falls silent and lets me get ahead. Seriously, how did we end up so different? At the car, she tosses her duffle in the back and settles, slumped, into the front passenger seat. The familiar quiet of my neighborhood passes until I reach the main drag. A few streets later, I turn into a more quaint area of town. It's even quieter and boasts an abundance of cloned two-story homes. Some are painted, but most are white, and all have the same awning and iron railing over a small front porch.

I stop in front of number twenty-six and unlock the car. "Have fun."

Amber responds by getting out and slamming her door and then slamming the back door after retrieving her duffle. Only my big brother instincts keep me from driving away before she's inside. The second her foot crosses that threshold, though, I burn cliché rubber.

Back on the main drag, I roll down the windows and let out a whoop. Phase one complete! Initializing phase two—date night, which naturally makes my palms sweat. I still can't believe Molly said yes to this party. It's a huge PDG. My whole body warms at the idea that she's comfortable because of me, that I'm able to do that for her.

Two red lights and a small traffic jam later, I turn down Molly's street. The sky is that perfect shade of sunset blue. Curse my timing. If Amber hadn't needed a ride, I would have gotten to Molly's in time to walk her to the car under this sky. Oh well. There's always next time, and if tonight goes at all like the last week has, there will be plenty of next times.

I pull into her driveway and kill the engine. A light upstairs turns off. Is that her leaving her bedroom? She might be walking down the stairs right now. Oh gods, what if her costume is just too gorgeous for words? She wouldn't tell me what it was, which left me to imagine all sorts of distracting options. My mouth goes dry, and I take deep breaths, which helps get my imagination under control. The party itself is more important than what Molly's wearing to it. This is her big reemergence back into the comfortable geek life. I'm not going to ruin that.

A curtain moves in the window beside the door. Is she spying on me? I can't help a smile as I get out of the car. She's adorable, adorable and worth every moment of my time as a gentleman. The stroll up the walkway and stairs is characterized by pointless shakes. There's nothing to be worried about. I look awesome. She, no doubt, looks awesome. I have the best gift ever for her.

It's time.

Chapter 22: Molly

I shove the Jedi robe back in my closet. I'm not wearing it. I don't need to wear it. There's nothing wrong with my costume, except that I'm not used to displaying this much skin. It's not my fault Wonder Woman doesn't wear a lot of fabric. It is my fault that she's the only girl costume that I didn't get rid of. Never mind that I've had a week to buy something new. I didn't, and it's a little late now. Craig will be here any minute, and I'm blushing.

Why am I blushing? It's not like he's never seen skin and legs before. Okay, Molls, breathe. Everything's going to be great. The funny part is that I'm not even worried about the geeky costume party with all the geeks. I'm worried about Craig liking my costume.

Seriously?

I close the closet before the Jedi robe makes another grab for my attention. Next is makeup. Eyeliner, hot pink lipstick, mascara, and blush—for when the natural one fades—complete my superhero look. Red heels are the next step—step, hah—and I slide my feet into red sandals as a car engine rumbles into range.

Is that him?

Yup, it's him. I step away from the window and put my hand to my heart. I look fine. He'll love it. It's time to get going before I lose my nerve. I turn off my bedroom light and practically fly down the stairs. Take that, invisible plane. In the living room, I peek through the curtains. Craig's car is in the driveway. He hasn't gotten out yet. What is he waiting for? Doesn't he know I'm having a heart attack in here?

As if he heard that question, a car door opens and closes, and then his footsteps are on the walkway, on the stairs, on the deck.

He knocks.

I inhale, which does nothing to calm my racing heart, and straighten my costume. The moment of truth is upon me. I take my time walking to the door, both to stall and because my legs shake. What if he's dressed as Captain America? We may as well just send a flag in our place.

I grip the doorknob. I've got this. One, two, three, and goodbye final barrier.

Craig is not Captain America. He's Spock. The most gorgeous Spock ever.

"Umm, hi." Umm, hi? Just tie me up with the golden lasso and toss me in the corner.

"Hey." His voice is soft, and he doesn't seem to notice my awkwardness. He runs his gaze slowly up my body, finally meeting my eyes. There's enough fire in them to burn the neighborhood down.

I gulp. Maybe I should go back for the Jedi robe.

"Nice costume." His voice is a little ragged, but nowhere near as husky as expected. Even so, the effect of my costume is clear in his expression, which makes me feel more powerful than it should. He gives his head a little shake and offers his arm.

169

"Shall we?"

I take it. "Sure." The rickety wood boards of the porch creek, and I teeter. What if they break?

"I've got ya." Craig slides an arm around my waist and pulls me against him.

That feels a little too good. I bite off a sigh when he releases me to open the car door. I maneuver my way into the vehicle, and he closes the door and comes around.

"Nice costume, by the way." I clasp my hands to hide their trembling.

He gives me a grin that would make my knees go out. "In honor of the movie that brought us together."

Is he trying to make me swoon? At this rate, I'm going to be sighing all over him before the end of the night. "Ah, natural twenty for relevance," I say instead of gushing about how sweet he is.

"Yeah." His ears turn a lovely shade of pink. He clears his throat. "I have something for you." He pulls a dice-patterned box out of his pocket and holds it out.

Oh geez. Talk about awkward. I push it back at him. "You didn't have to. I didn't get you anything."

"It's okay." He holds it firm. "Take. Open." His voice leaves no room for argument.

Well, I'm not going to ignore an order from Spock. I take the box and do as instructed. Inside, a bracelet made of dice rests on a pad of black velvet.

I suck in a breath. He got me a bracelet made of freaking dice. "Oh."

Craig grins, shy. "Do you like it?" There's so much hope in the words.

I take it out of the box, unclasp it and hold out my wrist. He fastens it in place, and I hold my arm up to catch the light. It shimmers.

"It's beautiful." I lower my arm. "And possibly the coolest thing I've ever seen. Thank you."

He takes my hand and kisses the back. "You're welcome. Ready to party?"

My skin tingles where his lips touched. The sensation runs up my arm, making me shiver. A kiss on the hand and a bracelet of dice. So far, this night is better than great. "Yeah."

He starts the car, plugs the party's address into his phone's GPS, and begins our journey into the unknown. We fill the drive with small talk, not the uncomfortable kind. The quaint, two-story homes of my neighborhood scoot by like a moving picture show from the 1930s.

"Are the others excited about this thing?" I say when we get on the main drag.

"Sonya sounded like it when I talked to her earlier. I haven't heard from Lyd, and Parker has a generalized excited emotion for just about every situation."

My stomach tightens at the mention of Lydia, and I force my expression to remain neutral. "You sound like you want to put Parker in rehab for that particular characteristic."

He laughs and, safely, merges into traffic. "Nah. Parker's just … an individual. His level of geekdom makes me look like a rank amateur."

"Hmm." It's all I can think to say. Lydia's heartbroken—because that's what it was—expression hovers at the edge of my mind. How am I going to keep quiet all night if she's upset? Maybe I should talk to her if I get the chance. Not that she'll probably want to talk to me. Rolls reversed, I'd avoid her like the mutated plague. This has disaster potential written all over it in glow-in-the-dark sludge.

Craig turns down a side street and slows to pay closer attention to the directions. Outside, the ambient lighting dims. Streetlights come farther apart, and residential lighting doesn't reach as far as the industrial-strength stuff on the main road.

In the sudden quiet, my obsessive thoughts about the Lydia situation magnify until they are echoing off the inside of my skull. "I'm surprised you need directions," I say in an attempt to drown out my thoughts.

"I don't frequent this neighborhood too often, and it's the kind with a billion turns to throw people off." He navigates one of said turns, only for the GPS to announce another one.

"So I see," I say and then keep talking because it's helping with my echoing thoughts. "I'm impressed that you aren't just driving around until you stumble across the right place."

He sticks his tongue out at me.

After a few more turns, the GPS announces our destination will be ahead on our left, which is interrupted by a horn blast behind us.

I yelp and lurch back, thwacking my head on the seat. "What the …?"

A dark-colored car drives up beside us. The passenger window rolls down to reveal Sonya dressed as Mary Jane. "Oh good. Now we don't have to walk in there alone."

"Always a perk," Craig says. He gestures around with one hand. "Have you seen free space to park?"

Sonya shakes her head. "We just got here, so text if you encounter a place." She rolls up her window, and the car moves forward.

Five minutes and a few texts later, we park behind Parker's car and closer to our final destination than I expected. The second Craig kills the engine, the butterflies erupt in my stomach. In only moments, we'll meet up with the others, including Lydia. The time for potential awkwardness is nigh.

"It'll be okay, you know," Craig says when we're on the sidewalk. "I'll be at your side all night."

"I know." The sentiment is appreciated, and as terrible as it is, I'm very glad for my recent fear of geek issues. As long as Craig attributes my nervousness to that, he won't attribute it to Lydia. That's incredibly selfish of me, but it makes me feel the tiniest bit better.

The driver's door of the other car opens, and Spiderman gets out. "Are we prepared to revel?" It's Parker. He and Sonya dressed to match. "Woo!" He strikes a pose—arms in the air, jazz fingers, and feet planted wide,

"Please, stop," Sonya says, coming up beside him. "It's bad enough that your name is Parker Peterson and you're dressed as Spiderman." She punches his stomach, and he deflates. "Don't embarrass yourself … or us."

Craig laughs. "Where's Lyd?"

"Not coming," Sonya says, adjusting her shirt. "Something came up."

The knot in my stomach unties itself. Talk about a stroke of luck. I don't have to try and keep my mouth shut all night. I don't have to fend off awkwardness the entire time. Pantheon, I'm going to Hell for some kind of unintentional emotional abuse. Is there even a circle for that?

Craig hums. "Okay. We ready?" But at least Craig will be next door in the circle for obliviousness.

"Indeed," Parker says. "Let us proceed." He struts down the sidewalk to the appropriate house, taking larger-than-necessary steps and swinging his arms.

Sonya blows out a breath and follows. "Mother Web, give me strength."

Craig and I take up the rear. When we reach the steps, an abbreviated version of my costume-party-going anxiety hits me. I should be shaking uncontrollably, but I just shrug. I'm protected here. Nothing can touch me. I am the Enterprise, and Scottie's got the shields up, thanks to my own personal Spock.

We climb the three steps and halt in a deformed line on the porch. Sonya knocks, and we wait. Bass to some pop song pounds through the house's walls.

"You have to knock louder," Parker says, raising his hand. "No one shall hear such a soft sound in such a loud place." He pulls back his arm as if he's getting ready to punch someone in the face and swings forward just as the door opens.

Parker flails forward, and Sonya catches him before he can cause a domino effect.

A guy dressed as some red-pantsed character I don't recognize stands in the doorway. He gives Parker a pointed look and then ushers us inside.

The temperature in the house is about twenty degrees warmer than outside. Colored lights blink from a side room. The music synchronizes to my heartbeat and pulses through my blood.

Craig slides his arm around my waist. Again, that feels too good. "Come on," he says, maneuvering me toward the room with the flashing lights. "Let's dance."

I stumble but keep moving. Dance? Like, in front of people? To pop music? We step into the next room. The flashing light is—as expected—a strobe, and the strobe—as expected—flicks over a bunch of twenty-somethings dancing. They all seem to have varying definitions of the term, however. The ones toward the center of the room jump and flop around like chew toys being mangled by dogs. Some on the outer edges have paired off into couples, and the ones toward the back have gotten personal.

Craig puts his lips to my ear. "Couple or flailing?"

The touch sends a shiver up my spine, but even so, I can't bring myself to say couple. The center mass of uncoordinated limbs calls to me. "Flail."

Craig's face lights up as if I just presented him with cheat codes to every game ever made. He leads the way onto the floor, and we flail around with the rest of our talentless type. After a few minutes, Sonya and Parker join us. Sonya's actually a decent dancer, but Parker .... Somewhere there's a kingdom of no-rhythm, and he's their long-lost ruler. It's a good thing for him, and everyone around him, that Spiderman doesn't wear a cape. The resulting disaster would not be pretty.

The club music finishes, and Hampton the Hamster starts squeak-singing about love. I grab Craig's shoulder and jump like a five-year-old who just opened her best Christmas present. He takes my hands and joins me. He actually joins my jump-squealing. If I wasn't sold, I am now. He didn't walk away. He didn't look at me like I was nuts. He's jumping and screaming the lyrics and butchering the tune with me.

"You know Spock would never engage in such illogical behavior, right?" I say over the techno-ish beat.

He taps his forehead. "There is no place for logic here."

Chapter 23: Craig

If I'd known Molly was this kind of a geek, I would have thrown a party weeks ago. The kid-grin on her face is the most beautiful thing I've ever seen. Not that mine is any smaller given how my cheeks are hurting. Crazy flailing dance moves will do that to a person, but it's worth it. Besides, no man worth his weight in gold pieces walks off the dance floor while there are Hamsters in love.

The song ends, and Powerline from *A Goofy Movie* takes over, belting about how we need to listen to one another's hearts. Molly and I make a circle with Sonya and Parker, and the four of us skip around like five-year-olds on sugar. I trip over the floor and burst out laughing. I can't remember the last time I had this much fun.

"You're a mess," Molly says and then throws her head back to sing along with the song's chorus.

I regain my balance, and for a minute, I just watch her. My heart skips a beat. Who is this girl? A couple of weeks ago, she'd been terrified to even think about being dorky. Now, she's in the middle of a party scream-singing the words to a Disney movie. I squeeze her hand and flail some more.

Goofy's laugh ends the song, and there's a lull. A few people ironically shout about how crappy the DJ is, and then the music starts again.

Beside me, Molly sucks in a breath. "I love Bryan Adams."

Sonya gives Parker a familiar look that means *no way* and waves to me. Parker follows, and Molly and I are left alone.

The song's intro resolves into Adams singing about the freedom of past years, and I hold out my hand to Molly. "May I have this dance?"

She responds by closing the distance between us and pressing against me. She rests her head on my shoulder, linking her fingers behind my neck, and suddenly, I'm flying. She feels amazing. I wrap my arms around her waist. The couple next to us is too close, so I move us to a more empty part of the floor and assume the circle-swaying movement that constitutes slow dancing at any high school or college-age event. Not that Molly seems to care. She nestles deeper into my arms and lets out a long breath. The cherry scent of her perfume tickles my nose, and I bury my nose in her hair. Adams is right. Heaven.

"Thank you," Molly says, tilting her head up so her chin rests on my shoulder.

Her breath on my neck sends a spine-shattering shiver down my back. "For what?"

"For being you. For helping me remember how much I love this." There's so much sincerity, so much gratitude in her voice.

Adams rocks the chorus, and his lyrics coupled with Molly's words sink into my blood, lighting me on fire. Of course I helped her. Hell, even if she hadn't been uncomfortable, I wouldn't have left her side tonight. Girl's claimed me, body and soul.

"Of course," I say and press my lips to hers. She gasps the tiniest bit, but I don't take the invitation. This isn't the time for an all-out kiss. I don't want an all-out kiss. This is a slow moment, and it will stay that way. I work my lips against hers, gentle. She goes still for a moment, and then she responds, featherlight and soft. The tenderness and trust in this kiss unwinds the muscles in my legs. Oh man, I can't. I pull back and gather her as close as I can. She leans into the embrace, and I tighten my hold, resting my cheek against her temple. The music is alive everywhere we touch, and it's all I can do to support my weight.

"Craig," she says into my ear, her voice barely a whisper.

That does it. I can't stand up anymore. I squeeze her waist and move to her side, leading us toward the wall and some chairs. My legs shake, making the trek almost impossible, and judging by the way she clings to me, hers do too.

She eases into a seat. Reluctantly, I let go of her and sit, offering my hand. She takes it and threads her fingers through mine. Adams fades out, and some typical club music—couldn't expect there to be none of that—comes on. I don't move. I'm perfectly content to sit here and hold Molly's hand for the rest of the night.

She rests her head on my shoulder. "Watching the dancing is oddly fun." Her voice is back to normal.

I know the feeling, and not just because a girl I really like is right next to me. "Always is. I don't know if there'll be another one of these anytime soon, but I'll go if you want."

She grins, and it lights up her eyes. "I'd like that." She stands and places my hand in my lap. "I'm going to run to the bathroom. Be right back."

"Okay," I say and watch her until she's out of sight around the corner. With nothing as pretty to look at, I crowd-watch. The music changes slightly, not that the floor does. The same people still press against the same people. It's kind of weird to stare at grinding, so I focus on costumes. The Hulk is in one corner with a girl on each arm, anime characters I don't recognize. To their left, the Wonder Twins are going at it, and I shudder. Don't even want to know.

Beside them, there are some Mortal Kombat characters mixed with the guys from Final Fantasy. Liu Kang turns from the group to pass a drink to Batman, who sips before handing it to his date. The girl, dressed as Lara Croft, takes a much longer swig, gives the glass back to Kang, and rolls her hips back into Batman. He stumbles but catches himself, settling both hands on her waist. They're like a train wreck. I can't take my eyes off them. He twists his hips, and Croft follows. Another few moves turn them so they face me. The girl's dark hair is pulled back in Croft's signature braid, revealing blood red lips, blue eyes, and an oval face I'd know anywhere.

My good mood wilts faster than a dead shrubbery. The music pounds in my ears. The rest of the room keeps moving. But I'm frozen in place. What is Amber doing here? I dropped her off at her friend's house. I watched her walk in the door. How did she get from there to this party, this party that has alcohol?

And what am I doing watching Bat Fella, who is at least twenty, dry hump my fifteen-year-old sister? Before I can think twice, I'm out of my chair and moving.

Amber rocks back into Batty again, eyes closed and an expression of ecstasy across her face. Batty flinches, the kind of flinch that comes with an aroused grunt, and slides his hand between her legs.

My vision turns red. Oh, hell no. No way is this happening. Not my sister. I draw myself to my full height and stomp across

179

the remaining space, knocking dancers aside. I get more than a few glares, but I'm way past caring. The distance stretches forever, but I reach my target and tap Batty's shoulder. "Mind if I cut in?" My voice is tight.

Amber's eyes fly open. For a second, the deer-in-the-headlights look on her face almost makes sneaking up on her funny, almost. She turns to Batty and says something I can't hear. Batty scowls at me and backs away.

"Thanks," Amber says, her voice a seductive purr. She stalks past me, gripping my arm hard enough to cut off circulation. I let her drag me. If she wants to think she's winning, fine, but that won't last.

Around the next corner, she lets go. "What are you doing here? Are you following me now? Spying for Mom and Dad?" Her voice pierces my ears like a dog whistle for humans.

For a second, I can only stare. Mom and Dad? As if they even know she's here. "I'm not spying on anyone. I was invited to this party. What are you doing here?"

"Partying." Righteous-teenager drips from the word like acid rain. "You know, that thing you rarely did, but I do all the time because I'm better at being a teenager than you ever were? See ya." She starts to storm away.

My older brother instincts kick into overdrive, and I block her path. "I don't think so. I might not be here to spy, but I'm not letting you stay. Have you even thought about what you'd do if there's trouble and someone calls the cops? You've been drinking."

She snorts, and it's a miracle smoke doesn't come out of her nose. "That is what the fake ID is for, brother mine. Now, go away and forget you saw me." She spins away.

Bad idea. I snag her braid and pull her back, ignoring her

screech of protest. "I don't like that plan, so here's a new one. We're leaving, now."

Chapter 24: Molly

I'm walking on air. This night is turning out to be better than I could have dreamed. The flailing, the slow dance— my legs are still ready to give out after that kiss. A shiver runs through me, coiling in my belly. I've never been kissed like that. If that's what dating Craig would be like, I'm there, no questions.

I knock on the bathroom door and listen. No one responds, so I let myself in and turn on the light. For a party, the place is pretty clean. I do my thing and cross to the sink. The girl in the mirror catches my attention while I wash my hands. She's smiling, and her hair is a bit of a mess from having fingers tangled in it. Her lips are still a little swollen from kissing, and her makeup needs a touch-up. I wink at my reflection and pull my lip gloss out of my purse, reapplying the hot pink and blowing myself a kiss.

"Nice look," I tell my reflection and then dry my hands and let myself out of the bathroom. A blonde girl dressed as some Greek god-type character pushes past me. "Move it."

I stumble and glare, but she slams the door in my face. A minute later, retching sounds come from the bathroom. Never mind. I'm good with being pushed aside.

I straighten my costume and stroll back down the hall to the main room. Some club music is playing, and most of the room is taking advantage. Spiderman and Mary Jane dance into my line of sight, grinding as if their lives depend on it. I'm frozen for a second until the girl turns, and it becomes obvious that it's not Sonya. That was its own brand of strange. Craig's going to love this story.

I leave Spidy and MJ to their business and start back toward the chairs. Craig isn't there.

That's odd. I stop and flatten against the nearest wall, letting a group pass. Maybe he went to the bathroom? Or maybe he went to get a drink. Either way, he'll probably be back in a minute. It's not like there's nothing to do while I wait. The dancing is evolving into an interesting porno—yippi. The Hulk and Liu Kang are passing a drink back and forth, and ... why are the Wonder Twins dirty dancing together? Pantheon, that's going to leave a mark. Out of self-preservation, I search for something less disturbing to watch. Blonde hair in Craig's shade catches my eye. Is he on the floor? Why would he be on the floor? Another group of oddly dressed people walk in front of me, and when they pass, there's Craig.

And some girl dressed as Lara Croft is leading him away.

All the air leaves my lungs, and my body goes weak. It's all I can do not to double over. Ward fills my vision, and no matter how hard I push, he won't go away. He was right. After everything I thought I overcame, after all the self-worth I thought Craig help me find, Ward was right. Craig's just like him. The second I walked away, he found the hottest thing in the room.

Croft pulls him into a hallway, and I dart for the front of the house. Everything blurs, and only then do I realize tears pour down my face. I swipe them away and keep moving. Don't stop. Don't slow down. Don't let him see you like this. He can't win. He can't know. God, I've been such an idiot. I never should have gotten close to him. No more geek guys, ever. They're all the same. They come off trustworthy and innocent because of their hobbies, and in the end, they're like every other guy. They just hide it better.

"Hey, Molly." Crap. Sonya.

I force my voice to come out cheery. "I'm just going to get some air. I'll be back."

She says something, but I don't hear. I'm moving—through the room, out the door, down the stairs. On the walkway, I pull my phone out of my purse and set a record calling Nikki. I can't stay here. I can't. I shouldn't have come at all. I raise the phone to my ear and pray for Nikki to pick up.

"Molly?" She answers on the first ring.

"Hi." My voice shakes. I clear my throat. "I need you to come get me."

"Are you okay?" Nikki's tone is frantic. Do I sound that bad? "Molls, are you hurt?"

"No, not physically." I sniff, gross. "I just … I can't—"

"I'm in the car. Where are you?"

She's the best. I give her the address—thankfully it's only a few blocks from her house—and hang up. What was I thinking coming to this party? I'm never going to learn. I'm not meant to be a geek. I'm not meant to have a happy geeky relationship. I wipe my eyes, and metal brushes against my cheek. The bracelet—more lies. I take the thing off and toss the worthless piece of crap aside. It's all been an act, and I fell for it, again.

True to her word, Nikki pulls up less than five minutes later, and I all but fly into the passenger seat.

Nikki takes one look at me and pulls me into an awkward one-armed car hug. "Jesus, what happened?"

I shrug out of the embrace. The tears are pouring down my face again. "I'll tell you. Just get away from here first."

She lets go and pulls a box of tissues from the bag of holding that is the backseat of her car. Now, that's the amount of tissues one should carry around. "Here. Buckle up." She faces forward and puts the car in gear. "We're going to my place."

"Okay." I sag against the seat and blow my nose. Lessons—I need to learn them, and they need to stick.

"So," Nikki says when we turn onto the next street. "What happened?"

I inhale. The story burns my lungs, but I have to get it out. "He's just like Ward." I tell her about the girl dressed as Lara and how he wasn't even trying to resist her.

"Prick," Nikki says. Then her shoulders sag. "It's a shame. You were happy with him."

I snort, which sounds as disgusting as the sniff. "Yeah, thrilled, especially when I saw him with the Croft look-alike."

"Well, obviously that wasn't happy." Nikki turns down another street and blows out a breath. "I meant before that. You've been practically bubbly lately, and you don't usually do bubbly. Things were going so well, and I don't know. He just seems different."

I give a bitter laugh. "Don't they all at first. Guys are all the same. Geek guys are no different."

Nikki purses her lips and shakes her head. "I don't know."

"Well, I do." I pull another tissue out of the pack and blow my nose. "I saw him go into an empty hallway with Lara Croft. Nothing good ever happens in empty hallways with girls in skimpy costumes."

185

"True." Nikki pulls into her family's driveway and turns the car off. She shakes her head again and opens her door. "I'm sorry, Molls. Do you want me to go back there and kick him in the nuts?"

I manage a weak laugh. "No. I don't want to think about him."

"That's a girl," Nikki says. "Now, let's get you hot chocolate and a sappy movie."

I nod and get out of the car. An invisible string tugs me back toward the party and the piece of my heart I left on the dance floor. My chest is somehow heavier without it, and I let out a breath. The feel of Craig's arms around me smothers and comforts me in the biggest paradox I've ever felt. I break free of the mental cocoon. There's no point in fantasizing about what I'll never have. If Ward was a critical miss, then Craig's a zero, and I'm done rolling for relationships.

Chapter 25: Craig

I shut the car off and pull the key before Amber makes a crazy lunge for it again. "Out."

She glares at me and folds her arms.

"Fine." I get out and hit the lock button. I practically parked on the grass to get as close to my house as possible. I'll worry about the landscaping later. "You can't go anywhere without the keys, and you can sit there all night for all I care." I slam the door and stalk toward the porch. Sure enough, the passenger door opens a minute later, and Amber joins me. I hit the lock again and march up the steps. There are still a ton of cars, and lights and laughter come from inside. We're interrupting the party, but I don't care. Maybe seeing Amber like this in front of their friends will get my parents to wake up.

"I hate you, you know." Amber's voice is venom.

I cram the key in the lock. "Yeah, yeah." A twist throws the bolt, and I push the door open. "Ladies first."

After a pause, she goes, and I follow, slamming the door and herding her toward the dining room.

As expected, Mom, Dad, and all their people are sitting around with Tupperware and booze. There isn't a sober eye in the place. I shove Amber through the doorway and block her exit. "I brought your daughter home," I say in a voice loud enough to wake dragons from an enchanted sleep.

"Thank you, honey," Mom says from the other end of the table. She glances my way and then does a double take. Some undefinable noise escapes her, and that does it. The entire room turns. Most of the guests shrug and go back to talking and drinking. A few study the newcomers—the girl in the skimpy clothes and Spock—commenting on *Star Trek*. One old guy, who is way too drunk, whistles.

By contrast, Mom and Dad just stare, jaws hanging.

Finally, I have their attention. I grip Amber's shoulder, point over my shoulder, and march back to the entryway. Behind me, Mom makes excuses to her guests. She'll be right back. Please, continue to enjoy yourselves. Whatever.

I pull Amber to a halt by the stairs and wait. A minute later, Mom and Dad join us, surprisingly steady for the amount of alcohol they've probably consumed.

"Amber Marie Lawrence," Dad folds his arms, "where did you get those clothes?"

"And where were you wearing them?" Mom says.

Unmysteriously, Amber develops situational laryngitis.

I, however, come down with no such affliction. "I was at a party. She was at the same party. There was alcohol and twenty-something guys with their hands on her."

Amber punches my shoulder. "So what? You're not my father."

"No," Dad says, stepping between Amber and me. "But I am. And this is your mother, and we are telling you, very rightfully, to get upstairs, stay upstairs, and get changed."

Amber throws her arms in the air. "What the hell? I'm not a kid. I'm fifteen years old."

Dad punches the banister. "Fifteen is less than eighteen. You are still a child, and you are acting about half your age. Upstairs, now!"

"Fine!" Yet again, she runs up the stairs, stomps down the hall, and slams her door.

In her wake, there's stillness and quiet, broken only by the chatter of the guests. Mom closes her eyes and rubs her temples. Dad just breathes, and I bask in my triumph.

After a long pause, Dad runs a hand through his blonde hair. "Jesus, what in hell just happened?"

That's my cue. I've been waiting for that kind of question as an opening to lay into them about responsibility and raising their daughter and doing their job as parents. The entire lecture is poised on the tip of my tongue, organized into topics and subtopics.

But none of it comes. I can't bring myself to yell at the people who raised me to be a decent human being. It's not my fault my less-than-rebellious teen years didn't prepare them for my sister, and really, I'm no better than Amber if I yell. What will yelling accomplish, anyway?

"She's feeling her outs." I slump against the banister and adopt a teaching tone. "She's not like me. She wants to party and be wild, and it's only going to get worse."

For the surprise of the century, my folks don't try to make excuses. They exchange a glance full of guilt and shake their heads in unison. Any other time, the synchronization would be creepy.

"Well," Dad says. "This has certainly been a wake-up call. Thank you for bringing her home, Craig. I don't …." He shudders.

I know that feeling. "Of course I brought her home, but I

can't keep being her parent. I need to get through the summer and finish school. I can't do that and watch over Amber."

"You won't have to." Mom pats my shoulder. "Starting tonight, that's our job. The party's over." She heads back toward the dining room.

Party. Molly. I've been gone too long. "I need to head back out."

"Go ahead," Dad says. "We'll see you later, and thank you again."

I shrug. "You're welcome again." My desire to throttle my folks has diminished. "It's what big brothers do, right?"

Dad half turns away. "It's what parents prevent big brothers from having to do."

Maybe this really did change things. I leave Dad standing at the bottom of the stairs and make my exit. Outside, the air is thinner. This has been a night of progress. My family's putting itself back together. Molly came to a geek party. Things are looking up.

My phone buzzes when I get to the bottom of the front steps. I pull it free and thumb it to life. There's a text from Parker, and the guilt comes back, ten times stronger. I need to tell Molly the truth about Amber. I kept my mouth shut with my folks for too long. Not telling Molly will only cause more problems, and if she doesn't want to be with me because I might have to play guard for my little sister, then that's how it is.

Never mind that my heart will crack in half. I shove the guilt away and open the text.

Can't find Molly.

The air isn't thin anymore. It's sludge, and it burns hotter than Dante's inferno. I force myself to take deep breaths. There are a lot of people at that party. He probably just means that he can't find her in the crowd. I text back, asking for clarification. The response comes almost immediately.

She's gone.

Gone? What does he mean, *gone?* My body goes limp. Only the need to get back there keeps me on my feet. I'm replying and running to the car at the same time. I even manage to unlock the car, open the door, and text at once. That's three-arm territory, but I do it. I nearly take out the neighbor's bushes backing out of my improvised parking spot, but plants are hardy. They'll be fine.

Molly might not be, though. Where is she? I stepped out for five minutes. I told Parker to find her and tell her I'd be right back. The house isn't that big. Even if they managed to miss each other, he should have found her by now. If he hasn't … I can't think about it.

I break some kind of time record getting from my house to the main drag and practically go double the speed limit the rest of the drive. Parker's reply comes as I'm turning onto the road where the party is. I don't bother to text back, just slam on the breaks and pull the worst parking job in history. I'm out of the car almost before I shut it off and sprinting toward the house.

Parker and Sonya are on the walkway, and tears pour down Sonya's cheeks.

"Craig." Her voice cracks. She rushes to my side and throws her arms around me, burying her face in my chest. "Oh my god, Craig, I'm sorry. It's all my fault."

I gather her in my arms and rub her back. "Sonya, calm down. What's your fault? What are you talking about?"

She doesn't respond right away, and every second of silence carves a hole in my chest.

"Molly," she says when her shakes calm a bit. "I saw her, said hi. She said she needed air, and I let her go. She came outside, and then Parker found me, told me about you and Amber. We came out here to tell Molly, and she was gone." She sags against me as if telling the story has taken all her energy. "Craig, it's dead out here. Some sicko could have come by, and ... oh God. Why did we even come to this thing? I don't even like parties." She starts crying again.

"It's all right. It's not your fault." And it's not, but it's not all right. This is way beyond all right. I keep one arm around Sonya and turn to search the surrounding area. Maybe there's a hint to where she went, anything.

Something glints in the grass halfway across the yard. I pat Sonya's shoulder and release her to check it out. It's probably nothing, but I'm beyond desperate. I reach the shiny object and crouch to find the dice bracelet lying in the dirt.

The sound I make is part dying werewolf, part raging cat. I grab the bracelet and am moving, not clear on where I'm going until I'm back at Sonya's side. "I gave her this tonight." My voice is hollow.

Sonya turns from Parker, who took up comfort duty. She takes one look at the bracelet and sinks to the ground.

I know the feeling. My legs threaten to give, and my vision blurs. Oh my god, if some sicko has his hands on her .... I ball my free hand into a fist and punch the porch railing. It's metal, so I don't get splinters. But my knuckles throb. Still, it's not enough. I punch it again and then again until Parker grabs my arm.

"Stop it." He wrenches it behind my back. "Doing that isn't helping. Call her. Maybe she wasn't feeling good and left."

"Without her bracelet?" I say.

"With what car?" Sonya says. "Face it, Parker, I screwed up."

"You didn't screw up. This is my fault." If I'd waited, if I'd told her myself …. Amber—if Molly's hurt, I'm going to kill my sister. That thought passes as fast as it comes. It's not Amber's fault. I need to do something.

I pull out my phone, call Molly, and wait. One ring, two ring. Come on, come on. Three, four.

"Hey, it's Molly. Leave a message, and I'll get back to you."

I do, telling her I'm back, that I don't know where she is, but if she's safe to call me. This happens twice more before I can't bear to hear her greeting again. After thirty seconds that feel more like a year, I send her a text saying the same thing. No response, no response.

"Should we call the police?" Sonya says.

"They won't do anything for a missing person until forty-eight hours pass," Parker says. It's a sign of how distraught he is that he's talking normally.

I nod. All I can do is stare at my phone and blame myself for being a good brother. That isn't something I should blame myself for. But this, this isn't okay. Molly could be hurt or worse, and I just left without telling her why.

My phone buzzes, and I almost drop it. All at once, I'm shaking like a leaf. Fingers fumbling, I navigate to the new text.

It's from Molly.

I let out the longest breath in history. "It's her." I open it and read.

Hey, this is Nikki. She's ok, but she's sleeping. I'll tell her ur lookin 4 her when she wakes up.

"Well?" Sonya says, back on her feet and leaning toward me like her life depends on it.

I don't know what to say. My jaw hangs open as if it's stuck in that position. She's with a friend? But why? Why did she leave? "She's at a friend's place."

Sonya stares for a minute and then rubs her eyes. "I'm done. I want to go home. Next time someone invites us to a party, remind me not to go."

"That makes two of us." Parker starts up the front steps. "I'll say our goodbyes." He goes back inside.

"Thanks," Sonya says and wanders toward Parker's car.

Again, I nod, not that anyone's paying attention, but my head's the only part of my body that will move. Did I do something wrong? She didn't even know what was going on, and she said she was having fun. Why would she just leave? The high of the last couple of weeks crashes like a level thirty fireball. The flames engulf me, burning all the happiness out of the memories.

"Craig?" Sonya says from a few feet away. "Are you okay?"

I stare at my phone for another minute and then shove it and the bracelet in my pocket. So much for a natural twenty on this relationship. "No," I say. And I don't know if I will be.

Chapter 26: Molly

Something bright shines in my eyes.

I roll over and bury my face in Craig's chest. His embrace is warm but not as firm as usual. He must be half asleep too. I snuggle farther into his arms and breathe him in.

"Molly," he says, though not gently. "Molly, come on." He shakes my shoulder.

I blink. At least I think I do, except he's disappearing. "No." The word comes out muffled, and I cling to him as if I'm drowning. "Don't go."

"I'm not going anywhere." That's not Craig's voice. That's a female voice. "Seriously, Molls, it's three in the afternoon, and I need to talk to you." It's a familiar female voice.

I open my eyes. No wonder Craig's chest felt soft. It's a pillow, and the light is the sun. Gasping, I roll over. I'm not in my room, but I know this place. The same pink curtains that have hung over the windows forever do nothing to block the outside light, and the light-green walls aren't helping, except to tell me where I am. It's the guest room at Nikki's. But why am I here?

"That's better." Speak of the devil, she's standing over me, hair and makeup done and hands on hips. Her very fake scowl fades, and concern floods her features. "I'm sorry I'm so impatient, but I've been trying to wake you up for ten minutes. Are you okay?"

Are you okay? Those three words unlock something in my head. The night before comes rushing back—the party, the girl dressed as Lara. Craig. I clamp down on the urge to cry or make some kind of Ewok noise and take a long, steady breath. "I guess I didn't dream it, then?"

Nikki shakes her head, but there's no pity in the gesture. "No, but I have news." She holds up my phone. "You got a text and a few voicemails from Craig. I responded to the text."

My heart pounds into my ears. "You what?" I lunge forward.

"Easy, feistypants." She holds the phone out of my reach and pins me with a withering stare. "I had a reason. Now, do you promise not to hurt me or the phone until you've read the text and listened to the voicemails?"

I clench and unclench my fingers. "Define *hurt.*"

"I'm serious, Molls." And she is. The joking Nikki who is so common in all situations doesn't even attempt an appearance. "Read and listen. If you want to punch me afterwards, fine." She holds out the phone. "But do this first, okay?"

I stare at the phone. Nikki admitted it's Craig, but she's not cursing him out or saying all men are scum. Does that mean it's not that bad? What if she just doesn't realize how bad it is? What if I read it, understand it in a way she didn't, and fall apart again? The image of him following Croft off the floor blares like a red alert in my brain. The shields are down. The ship is hit, and it's time to evacuate. I run for the pods.

But something stops me. The calm voice of the emergency steering system tells me there's a chance to save everyone. I hesitate, but I run back. What kind of captain would I be if I didn't at least try?

"Okay." I take the phone, which is open to my text messages. Craig is at the top of the list. My stomach gives an involuntary heave. Fingers shaking, I select the conversation. The texts from the past week scroll to the bottom, but sure enough, there are two messages I don't recognize with time stamps for last night.

Craig: *Molly, it's Craig.* Cuz I don't know that. *Where are u? Really, I'm not joking. We can't find you, and I'm scared. Text or call if u get this.*

I read Nikki's reply—thank God she said it was her talking— and close the message. Scared, really? Was that before or after he stuck his hand, or something else .... Stop it, Molls. Listen to the voicemails. Then get angry.

I close the text with stabbing motions and switch to voice-mail. There are three new ones with timestamps of last night. I select the first and hold the phone to my ear.

"Molly." Craig's voice, frantic, explodes from the speaker, cutting off my thoughts. "Molly, it's me. Where are you? We can't find you, and Sonya said you came out for air. And you're not here, and if someone grabbed you ..." There's a moment of silence and a shaky breath. "Just call me if you get this."

I bite down on the inside of my mouth. It sounds like someone shredded his vocal cords.

The next two are even worse, and when Craig's hysterical tone ends the last with a desperate plea for me to respond, my hand falls into my lap. It's as if I don't have enough strength to hold it up anymore. He ran around looking for me? But I saw him with Lara Croft.

"Do you still want to hit me?" Nikki says.

I blink a few times. Hit her? No. Figure things out, yes. My head is reeling. "I don't understand."

Nikki snorts. "Funny, cuz I do." She points to my phone. "Something else happened last night, and you need to talk to him."

More stomach heaving. "I can't." I left and slept until three the following day. I never sleep that late. This nearly destroyed me, and Nikki wants me to talk to him? Whose side is she on, anyway? "What if it's all an act? What if I fall for it again?"

"Honey, I heard that voicemail. That was no act."

My gut agrees, but my brain isn't done. "Okay, maybe not, but I just can't. If it is, if I was wrong, I can't handle it. I can't handle another Ward. I—"

"Molls." Nikki grabs my phone and tosses it on the night-stand before sitting next to me, grabbing my chin and forcing me to make eye contact. "I know Ward hurt you, bad. But that was doomed before it started. You weren't happy with him, and he was a player. He lied and cheated. He said he would change for you, but people don't change. Craig isn't Ward."

I try to shake my head, but Nikki's grip is solid. My heart wants to believe so bad. There are just too many buts. "I don't know." My voice is small.

"Well, I think I do, and I think he deserves another chance. Text him. Tell him you want to meet somewhere public. Then if things don't go well, you have an escape." She puts my phone in my hand.

I stare at it, waiting for it to bite. After a minute, no mini plastic teeth dig into my skin. "You really think I should?"

Nikki smiles. "I do, but it's up to you." She releases my face and stands. "I need to finish getting ready for work. If you wanna get dressed, I can drop you home on the way."

With that, she leaves, and I'm left with my thoughts and a too-quiet room. The phone seems to weigh a thousand pounds. My fingers twitch, the little traitors. Clearly, a part of me wants to text him, but a big part of me wants to run, not walk, to the nearest escape hatch. He walked off with that girl while I was in the bathroom. He betrayed me.

Those words don't ring true, though. My heart refuses to accept them. Maybe that's how I know. Maybe it's that little tug that's telling me there's more here than I realize. Loathed as I am to admit it, Nikki's right about Ward. It never would have worked. And Craig isn't Ward. He's a different person, a good person. He's someone I'm starting to trust and, more importantly, that I want to trust. Trust is a two-way street, though, and I can't expect to get it if I don't give a little in return.

"You better be right about this, Nikki," I say to the empty space and unlock my phone.

Chapter 27: Craig

I hop onto a barstool and wait. For a Sunday afternoon, A's isn't too crowded, which is good. This is going to be interesting enough without a huge audience.

A couple at a booth across from me stops perusing the menu to engage in an all-out make-out. I grit my teeth and turn away. I don't wanna watch that, and I really don't wanna be accidentally staring at it when Molly shows up.

If she shows up, and if I want her to show up. Yes, my heart did Pegasus-worthy loop-the-loops when she texted me yesterday, but they didn't last. Doubts and the beginnings of anger replaced them. I don't know why she left the party, and only my overwhelming curiosity got me to this meeting. My overall reaction will depend heavily on her story.

And I don't know what I want the outcome to be.

"Mind if I join you?" If only summoning spells were this reliable. Molly slides onto the stool beside me. She's not dressed in work attire, which means nothing, and her voice is guarded. Her hair is in a simple ponytail, and both makeup and emotion put a mask on her expression.

"I'd say you already have." I go silent and wait. This is her deal, not mine.

She flushes and stares at the drink fountains. "Thanks for coming."

I shrug. "You're welcome." This is off to a great start.

She chews on her lower lip. After another eternity, she faces me. "I'm sorry. I thought talking in here would be good, but it's not." She slides off the stool. "Can we go out back?"

Fine by me. I stand and flail my hand in a general after-you gesture. "Lead on."

She does. We leave through the main door and take a right around the outdoor seating area. There's no one there, and she takes me around the next right, which brings us between A's and whatever store is beside it. Another few feet sees us at the loading dock, and she stops and faces me.

I put the hypothetical brakes on about five feet away and wait, hands in pockets.

She opens and closes her mouth. "I …" She swallows and, with a deep breath that seems to take everything she has, meets my gaze. "I'm sorry I disappeared last night."

I nod. I gathered as much from the fact that she wanted to meet, but I don't say that. That's just mean, and the angry part of me doesn't want to be quite that nasty.

She breathes again. "Do you remember the talk about how Ward and I broke up?"

Of course I do. But what does that have to do with this? "Yeah."

"Well, I didn't tell you the whole story." She leans back against the wall and stares at the ground. "We were together for two years, and I thought everything was great. I really thought we were going somewhere." Tears form in her eyes, but they don't fall. "I was really wrong. He, he ended our relationship by letting me find him in a hallway at a party with a half-naked girl."

The words punch me in the stomach. Good God, Ward really is, as Lyd put it, the dickiest dick who ever dicked. "That sucks, but—"

"There's more." She holds up a hand. "That girl, well. Ward always had a thing for cosplay, especially videogame cosplay. The girl he was with that night was dressed as Lara Croft, and he'd flirted with girls dressed as Lara before, right in front of me and without caring that I was upset." She clasps her hands. "So when I saw that girl dressed as Lara dragging you away last night, and you weren't even trying to resist …."

It takes me a minute to understand the implications of the situation. Oh wow, it really was Amber's fault. Well, not her fault, but she's directly involved. This entire thing is a giant misunderstanding, which would have been avoided if I'd just told her about my sister problems sooner. Well, it's time to come clean and deal with the consequences. "That girl wasn't dragging me off for any good reasons, trust me." I let out the breath. "In fact, if that girl ever speaks to me again, it will be a miracle."

She tenses, gaze darting around, and I realize how that must have sounded.

"Molly." I close a bit of the distance between us. "That girl was my sister."

The mask over her emotions falls faster than a dark god from grace. For a moment, she's with me, right in front of me. Curiosity, relief, happiness—they fill her eyes. There's more, though. There's hope. It's written across her face. She wants to believe.

And I want her to. Seeing all those emotions in her eyes lifts the dark cloud over my heart. Not knowing where I stood with her the last two days killed me a little inside. I've never wanted to be there for someone like I want to be there for her, and the thought of walking away leaves me hollow. Ward had a grip on her jugular, and it took her more than one battle to dislodge him. I can't hold that against her.

"Remember when I mentioned that my sister is rebellious? Well, I didn't realize just how rebellious Amber is until last night. She's fifteen, and when I saw some guy trying to take advantage of her on the dance floor ..." The fire builds in my chest again. I douse it as best I can. "I dragged her home and had it out with my parents. I told Parker to tell you I'd be back, but you must have left before he found you. It was a giant mess of bad timing. I should have waited the thirty seconds to tell you myself, but I couldn't see past my fear for my little sister. I'm sorry." As if telling her saps my energy, I sag. It's done. She can respond however she wants.

"No," she says almost immediately. "I'm sorry. If I'd followed you and confronted you, this wouldn't have happened. I was just so scared, but I don't want to be scared anymore." She steps closer. "I really like you, Craig. You're not Ward, and you're not the losers before Ward. I can't be mad at you for taking care of your sister, and I caused a problem last night because I couldn't deal with maybe being wrong about you."

"We both could have done better." I finish closing the distance and circle my arms around her waist. "And we will because nothing about you and me in the same place is wrong." I brush my lips to hers, and her phone rings.

Her phone rings?

Seriously, this is my life. I move away but keep my arms around her. "You should get that."

She's still for a minute. Then, with an extremely despondent sigh, she pulls out her phone. The easy calm she managed in the last few minutes vanishes, replaced by all-out tension.

"Everything okay?"

She shrugs. "Not sure, but I have to take this."

I release her and step back. "Go ahead."

She answers the call. "Hello?" The word seems to drag.

I lean back on my heels. This isn't looking good, but whatever it is, I'll be here for her. Nothing's going to ruin this moment.

"Oh," Molly says, and her smile is bright enough to eclipse the sun. "Yes. Yes, I can. Thank you very much. Have a good day." She hangs up and shoves her phone in her purse. "That was one of the places I applied to work."

The tension bubble in my chest pops. "You got it?"

She throws her arms around me. "I got it."

I'm not sure who kisses who first, but next thing I know, we're against the building. And it feels good, too good. There's an electric current between us, and it's us together, going boldly into the future. Together.

Finally, I pull back and rest my forehead against hers. "Congratulations."

"Thank you." She kisses my nose and squirms out from between me and the wall. "Now, correct me if I'm wrong, but there's an M and M session happening now."

"There is." And I'm being shoved aside for it? That should hurt, but it doesn't. There will be plenty of time. M and M will not wait for rogue or shaman. "You sure you want to go?"

"Yes. It's the perfect way to celebrate. Besides," a devilish spark glints in her eyes, "I'm so close to beating you to level three."

I'm at her side in two strides, tickling her. She squeals, and I scoop her into my arms and carry her back toward the front of the restaurant. "Let me make something perfectly clear," I say when we reach my car. I put her down and grip her shoulders. "You are not beating me to level three."

"We'll see about that." She jogs around to the passenger side, gives me a wink, and gets in.

My heart melts the littlest bit. I'm so gone, but I couldn't care less. This is the best feeling in the world.

The drive to Dawn's place is filled with the flirty banter I've waited for between Molls and me. I park and lead the way to the door, where I punch the code to ring the apartment. Dawn buzzes us in, and we race upstairs. She beats me by elbowing my stomach on the landing, and we dash to Dawn's apartment, where I knock. There's a minute of us bouncing on our heels before Dawn lets us in.

"You are late," she says, glancing between us.

I push my way inside. "I know. Just make sure I get to level three before she does."

Molly punches my shoulder.

"About time," Sonya says when I rush into the game room. Her gaze lands on Molly, and she looks at me with a wide-eyed question.

I nod, telling her all is well, and pull out a chair for Molly and then sit beside her. "What did we miss?"

"Our eminent death," Parker announces.

"The Puff creature speaks the truth," Dawn says. "Roll initiative. You are under attack."

"Of course we are." Molly digs her dice out of her purse.

"I'll get mine out in a sec." I grab Parker's D20, and my palms go sweaty. That's an overreaction to an initiative roll if I've ever had one. Dice, don't fail me now.

The crackle of Molly's die hitting the table interrupts my concentration. "Seventeen."

I blow out a breath. Now or never. Squeezing my eyes shut, I let the D20 fall.

Sonya makes some kind of squeaking noise.

I open my eyes.

I rolled a twenty.

"Critical success," Dawn says. "And you attack first."

I stare at the twenty—that glorious number—and then grab Molly's hand and squeeze. "Critical success, indeed."

Continue The Games of Love with
ONE FLING TO RULE THEM ALL

The fun continues with Lydia's story in **ONE FLING TO RULE THEM ALL!**

It began with the forging of a great friendship.

For too long, Lydia Bell has been caught in the bittersweet grip of unrequited love for her best friend. When fate throws her into the path of Scott Henderson, a fellow soul nursing the sting of rejection, unexpected sparks fly like flaming arrows. A fling seems like the perfect salve for their shattered hearts, and desperate to move on, they agree it's worth a try.

But as it turns out, they are both terrible at flings. And what happens when they start falling (not into a fiery mountain, thankfully) for each other?

Follow Lydia and Scott on their mostly epic quest for love. Filled with witty banter, heartwarming friendship, and all the geeky moments you could ask for, **ONE FLING TO RULE THEM ALL** is the perfect journey for the armchair adventurer in all of us. No actual life-risking required. To grab your copy from your retailer of choice and for more about The Games of Love series, visit https://kitnkabookle.com/the-games-of-love/.

Acknowledgements

I originally wrote and published this book back in 2015, and while I have people to thank from way back when, the list has grown and changed, so here we go for an extended acknowledgements section, if you will.

It's been a long road of writing and publishing, giving up, and finding my way back here. It's been an even longer road finally deciding to do something with this book and series (well, other than watch it sink to the bottom of the sales ranks, never to rise again). So with that in mind, I first need to thank the Writing Popular Fiction program at Seton Hill. I workshopped the first three chapters of Critical Hit-On at my final residency, and the response was an hour of fan-squealing that gave me the initial confidence I needed to push forward. So a big thank-you to everyone in that critique session.

When I first wrote this, I was living in North Carolina and had a host of other writers I hung out with. A big thanks to them for reading this in its early form and giving me feedback. In particular, thank you for your notes about Molly's character. She didn't quite feel like a person until I incorporated your feedback.

A super huge thanks to Dave D for gifting me digital copies of every Dungeons and Dragons book you own and also for helping me figure out what types of characters to have, well, my characters play in M and M. My specialty in gaming lies more in the "I will deal damage from 30 paces away," not logistics, so you have no idea how helpful you were.

To Stephanie, the lovely editor who proofread this way back in the day, thank you for your attention to detail and for telling me you loved the book. That was another "I can really do this" boost that I very much needed.

I was living with my parents when I initially wrote this, and while that is no longer the case, I'd be remiss if I didn't thank them for keeping me fed and at least a little calmer than usual while I ran around yelling about how "I'll never finish this book!" For the intervening years, thanks for never giving up on this series. I did for a while, and I'm sure you asking me about it periodically got me thinking enough to actually revamp it.

As mentioned, I'm no longer living with my parents. Now, I live with an amazing partner and his daughter, whom is my "Little Fish." The two of them have at least partly taken over keeping me fed, though I've also learned to remember to eat without prompting. Thank you both for putting up with me muttering and wandering around the house as a way to work out plot holes. A specific thanks to Dave (the partner) for being around to bounce ideas either about stories or the publishing process. This is a big journey to take on my own, so having someone to talk to about it is very helpful.

And finally, thank you, readers. Thank you for loving pop culture and geek stuff and humor and for reading books. Thank you for existing so I have someone to put these stories in front of. Thank you for sharing my interests so I can write little Easter egg inside jokes into the text and know that someone will get them. Thank you for your support (can't be thankful enough for that) and your time and your love of reading.

About the Author

Born a New Englander, M.T. DeSantis moved south in early adulthood, realized she actually liked winter, and promptly moved back north. She's currently trying out life as a Michigander/anian with her family, who also (mostly) actually like winter. When not making word magic, M.T. can be found practicing yoga, attempting to make friends with the oven, or trying to read while people keep talking to her. For more from M.T., visit https://books.bookfunnel.com/mtdesantis, where you can grab some free stories and sign up for her periodic newsletter, in which she makes lovely announcements about books and stuff.

Also by M.T. DeSantis

Books in Grimmfay (dark, fairy-tale circus)
Grimmfay
Once Upon a Broken Sky

Books in The Games of Love (fun and flirty no-steam romances)
Critical Hit-On
One Fling to Rule Them All
Finish Him
Love in Geek Minor (to be released)
Fake It So (to be released)

Other Stories
To Love a Beast (short high fantasy Beauty and the Beast retelling)